THE LORD'S ACRE

The Sabine Series in Literature
SERIES EDITOR: J. BRUCE FULLER

The Sabine Series in Literature highlights work by authors born in or
working in Eastern Texas and/or Louisiana. There are no thematic
restrictions; Texas Review Press seeks the best writing possible by
authors from this unique region of the American South.

Books in this Series:

Cody Smith, *Gulf*
David Armand, *The Lord's Acre*
Ron Rozelle, *Leaving the Country of Sin*

THE LORD'S ACRE   A NOVEL   DAVID ARMAND

Huntsville • Texas

Published by Texas Review Press
Huntsville, TX 77341

Printed in the United States of America

Library of Congress Cataloging in Publication Data

Names: Armand, David, 1980– author.
Title: The Lord's Acre : a novel / David Armand.
Other titles: Sabine series in literature.
Description: Huntsville : Texas Review Press, [2020] | Series: The Sabine
    series in literature
Identifiers: LCCN 2020004456 (print) | LCCN 2020004457 (ebook) |
    ISBN 9781680032208 (paperback) | ISBN 9781680032215 (ebook)
Subjects: LCSH: Dysfunctional families—Louisiana—Fiction. | Reli-
    gious leaders—Louisiana—Fiction. | Faith—Fiction. | Louisiana—
    Social life and customs—Fiction.
Classification: LCC PS3601.R55 L67 2020 (print) | LCC PS3601.R55
    (ebook) | DDC 813/.6—dc23
LC record available at https://lccn.loc.gov/2020004456
LC ebook record available at https://lccn.loc.gov/2020004457

Cover photo courtesy Alistair Hamilton / Flickr

this book is dedicated to my wife

"But the men marveled, saying,
'What manner of man is this, that even
the winds and the sea obey him!'"

CONTENTS

It's about one-thirty in the morning. Quiet. And I'm the only one back here. Crouched behind the old Sunflower grocery store in the middle of Folsom, Louisiana, a little hamlet just south of where I grew up. I'm kneeling on a dark square of oily asphalt with a flashlight pointed in front of me, looking for a way to pry my way in.

The flickering white light skips across the cinder-block wall behind the store, finally landing on the entry point I've been looking for. I stop first, then listen for the sounds of a police cruiser easing down the gravel lane behind me or otherwise someone coming up on foot, their heavy boots crunching over the rocks before they finally grab me by my shirt collar. A set of thick hairy fingers against my neck, the cold metal of handcuffs locking shut around my wrists.

But things are quiet. Still. Calm, save for my thudding heart.

I sit there for a minute, hunched over in the dark, the pea gravel stabbing at my knees, my flashlight pressed between my shoulder blade and cheek as I pick up the crowbar from where I had set it down next to my boots. I start working on the back door with it. It's the only thing keeping me from getting inside the store now. That, and maybe my fear of getting caught.

My flashlight's white beam skates across my hands as I work on the door. Prying, prying. I can hear it worrying against the threshold until it finally comes loose. Then I look around again to make sure no one sees me. I wait a minute to see if an alarm sounds. None does.

So I open the door and aim my light into the store. I put the crowbar back in my pants— through my belt loop so that it hangs down against the side of my leg like a cop's baton—and then I walk inside. I gentle the door shut behind me.

Inside the store it's almost completely dark, save for the weak beam of my quivering flashlight. I hold it up, scan the store with it, then walk down one of the aisles toward the back where the manager's office is. It's in a raised area toward the rear of the store, and it has wainscoted walls enclosing it on all sides. There's a long narrow window across the front, through which I imagine the manager looks out on his store as customers go up and down the aisles.

The office is fronted by a flimsy wooden door, which is plastered over with a large calendar and an advertisement for Purina dog food.

It's nothing for me to pry it open. The wooden frame splinters against the metal edge of my crowbar.

I walk into the dusty office and I'm about to look for the stack of black plastic cash register tills which I know must be there—either that or a safe, someplace where all the money is kept—when the beam of someone else's flashlight lands on me. And now I'm standing directly under the wash of its bright and accusing light.

"Stop," comes a voice from somewhere out of the darkness, from just behind that bright beam of light. "Don't you even think about moving," it says.

I don't know what to do. So I just drop my flashlight and the crowbar I had been holding onto the floor and put my hands over my head. I stand there. I know that it's far too late for me to do anything else.

1

The house where I lived when I was a kid was in Angie, Louisiana, and it was situated at the edge of a large field that was pocked with cows and horses. There was a barbed-wire fence surrounding us that had cattle guards in the openings to keep the livestock out of our yard. But those animals weren't ours anyway. My dad leased that little piece of land and the tiny house it was on from a man named Mr. Tally, and he worked on Mr. Tally's farm to cut down on the cost of the rent—or sometimes to cover the rent entirely, depending on how much work he did in a given month. It seemed like a decent arrangement to me, but my dad seemed unhappy about it. I think his pride at living on another man's land bothered him.

The longer we lived out there in the pasture, the more miserable my dad seemed to become. My mom too. She was getting more and more restless and unhappy, dreamy almost. Like she was completely checked out from reality. It was as though, like my dad, she envisioned her life much differently than how it had turned out thus far. I know this because she often told me so, which made me feel like an impediment to her happiness, as if my very existence was slowing her down.

So I spent a lot of time alone, away from my parents, whenever I could. Sitting out in the woods and listening to the animals in the nearby pasture. Daydreaming about another life. I had some old sacks of horse feed that I sliced up one time with a pair of scissors, which I then strung to tree branches like a canopy, making a bed of sweet-smelling hay beneath their flickering shade. I would lie in these nests day after day. Making up stories, talking to myself. The other kids who lived around us thought I was strange, and unless they were bored or desperate, they mostly stayed away from me. I had no friends to speak of.

3

One day after I had spent most of the afternoon sitting in the woods like I usually did—listening to the animals and staring up at the sun until my eyes burned, then closing them and watching the spots erupt on the backs of my eyelids, the purple and orange shapes moving around the circuits of capillaries like the viscera in the lava lamp my mother kept on her nightstand, the tiny veins probably exploding in irreparable ways I couldn't have known about then—I heard my mother calling me. Instead of answering her, I just got up and walked back to the house to see what she wanted. I didn't have anything better to do.

When I got there she was standing on the porch holding a brown envelope from the homeschooling group we belonged to. This was mainly to assuage my parents' anxiety about truancy officers, which, in a place like Angie, I don't think even existed. We never went to any homeschool meetings and I never studied with other kids. Being a part of the group was just a formality, my parents had told me, a way to keep Big Brother off our backs.

She handed me the envelope. Inside was a letter announcing a contest for the "Just Say No" campaign, something First Lady Nancy Reagan had initiated to keep kids like me off of drugs, it said. The letter also said that I was invited to come up with a creative response to what it meant to me, personally, to "Just Say No."

I had never thought about anything like that before. I had never even seen any drugs in my life, unless the pills my mother kept in her bathroom counted as drugs. I certainly never took any of them, though, nor had I ever felt compelled to. I was only twelve years old.

"Do you want to enter?" my mother asked from where she stood on the porch, looking down at me.

"Um, I don't know," I said. "What would I do?"

"You can do anything you want. It says you can write a poem. Draw a picture. It looks like the only guidelines are saying no to drugs."

She laughed at that last part, as though the notion were silly. But I could tell she was interested in the creative aspect of the proposal. I was surprised, though, as the letter said this was a school-board-sponsored event, to be underwritten by the federal government; and both my parents despised the school board, as well as the federal government. In fact, they despised any form of organized governing bodies, which is one of the reasons why they home-schooled me in the first place.

"Okay," I told her.

Probably sensing my complete lack of enthusiasm, my mother asked me if I was sure. "You don't have to," she said. "I just thought it might be interesting. Give you something to do with your time. Lord knows you have lots of it."

"Yeah," I said. "I guess I'll do it. Does it say what you get if you win?"

"A hundred dollars," she said. "So you better make it good." She laughed again. "I'm sure you have some stiff competition around here."

I didn't have to look at my mother's face to know she was being sarcastic. I could hear it in the way she pronounced the last words of her sentence, as though she had been born and raised in the country. Like so many other things were to her, my mother thought our life here was provincial. Misery-inducing. She wanted to live in New Orleans, she'd often say, but my dad insisted the city was no place to raise a child. So here we were.

"I'll try my best," I said.

2

I ended up drawing a comic strip with the worn-down stubs of some colored pencils I found lying among the mess of strewn-about clothes and papers, which seemed to erupt from every partially closed drawer and blanketed nearly every messy surface of our house.

The comic was simple: it depicted two older boys trying to get a younger boy to take some drugs, which I imagined as a bunch of little red and blue circles in their palms. The little boy (whom I thought of as myself) simply told the two older kids "no" as they held out their hands and looked down menacingly at him. Finally, the last frames showed the little boy going to his teacher and informing her of the older boys' evil intentions. The blue-haired teacher praised the boy with a pat on the shoulder. The final square was overlaid with thick gray lines, the two drug dealers standing sadly behind them, their fingers wrapped around the metal bars as though they were holding on to one of those batons you pass back and forth in a relay race. My story was simple, but it was the best I could do.

When I showed the comic to my mother, however, she criticized it, pointing out how it was unrealistic and that no older kid would waste his drugs on a child like that. I had fallen for our government's fear-inducing propaganda, she said. I had done exactly what they wanted me to do, thought exactly what they had wanted me to think. She said she was disappointed but not surprised.

Then she laughed at me. I was crushed.

What was weird is that normally I would have been discouraged by my mother's criticism—enough to just throw the drawing away and forget about the contest. But something in replaying her mean-spirited laughter over and over in my head that night made me put the comic in the return envelope and mail it off anyway. I never bothered to show it to my dad; I just figured his reaction would be the same as my mother's, if not worse.

There was a small part of me, I think, that submitted the drawing to spite my parents, even though I never thought I actually had a chance of winning. Just putting it in the rusty mailbox in the first place was an act of rebellion, a small defiance.

I did take my mother's criticisms to heart, though, and I had believed her when she said that my story was sad and pathetic. In fact, her laughter was still ringing in my ears when, a few weeks later, I got a letter in the mail that said my comic strip had won first place among all the entries from Washington Parish—not just the home-schooled students, but the real ones too. I couldn't believe it.

At first I thought it was a joke. Until I saw that the letter was signed by the superintendent of public schools in Washington Parish; there was even a raised seal beneath the swirling black ink of his name. I rubbed my index finger over it, imagined this important man in his office admiring my artwork, something I created, and then signing the letter and stamping it to make it official, to legitimize for the first time in my life something that I had done.

There was a postscript, too, that said my comic would be displayed with a blue ribbon next to it at the Washington Parish Free Fair that weekend. The superintendent said he hoped he'd see my parents and me there to help us celebrate my accomplishment.

"Can we go?" I asked after showing the letter to my parents and watching their straight and serious faces as they read over it.

"I don't know, Eli," my dad said. "Those fairs are bad places. They encourage gambling. They represent the basest of human experience. You wouldn't believe the people who go to those things. When did you enter a contest anyway?" he said. "Why didn't I know about this?"

"You're never here, John," my mother said.

My dad just rolled his eyes, looked down at me sternly.

"I don't know, son," he finally said. "We'll think about it."

This, I knew from past experience, usually just meant "no."

As I slouched on the sofa where I sat across from my parents, I thought about the fact that neither one of them had congratulated me. In fact, they seemed betrayed that I had sent the comic strip off in the first place, and even further betrayed by the public school system—a place that they always claimed encouraged mediocrity and conformity. That's why they home-schooled me, they said. They didn't want me to think like everyone else. And here I was, they said, doing exactly that.

My parents went on to ask me if I really believed the story I had written. Would I really react the way the protagonist did in my comic? I didn't even know what the word "protagonist" meant, so I just pretended to understand them. They said they both imagined that, in reality, I'd probably take the drugs that were offered to me, even though I was barely even thirteen years old. That I was simply too influenced by our corrupt culture, despite their efforts to shield me from it. We needed to start going back to church, my dad had said. My mother agreed with him. It had been too long—I was backsliding, and it was their fault. I started to wish I had never put that envelope in our rusted-out mailbox, had never raised the little metal flag so that the mailman would pick it up. What had I been thinking?

3

Despite my regret, though, and despite all of my parents' empty threats—as well as their mutual diminishing of my success—they were both more than willing to drive me into town the next day in order to collect my one-hundred-dollar prize money, which my award letter had said was being donated by the owner of Ray's Drive-In, a little diner in town and one of the sponsors for the award that year.

I still remember walking into the restaurant with my parents that afternoon. How it smelled inside. The hamburgers and fried-shrimp Po'boys, the sound of the malt machine stirring up thick vanilla ice cream, the pinball machine and the Pac-Man arcade game next to it. My parents had never taken me there before (they thought the food was "poison") but, this time, they said it would be okay. Only to get the money, though. We would order no food. No poison.

At home we would eat fresh eggs from the chickens that wandered around our yard—and sometimes the chickens themselves—vegetables from the ever-sprawling garden that my dad surrounded our house with, tofu, bean sprouts. Places like Ray's, my parents would tell me, were what made Americans so ill. We were better than that, they said. Our bodies were our temples and we had to treat them accordingly.

When my mom and dad and I walked up to the counter of Ray's that afternoon, my mother spoke for me, telling the girl behind the register that I had won the "Just Say No" drawing contest and that we were there to collect my money. My dad didn't say anything. He was looking around the restaurant disapprovingly, likely thinking how much better and more enlightened he was than everyone else in there.

"Congratulations," the girl said, looking down at me after my mother had finished talking. I didn't make eye contact with her and I could feel my face flush at the very sound of her voice. She looked about fifteen or sixteen, I think, and she was pretty. Long, brown hair pulled back into a ponytail. Pale, freckled cheeks and large blue eyes. Her smile was warm and unguarded. Her nametag said "Heather Anne."

"Thanks," I mumbled, looking at the countertop instead of at her.

"Well, let me go run back and get Mr. Ray," she said. "He wants to meet you and congratulate you himself. Plus he's gotta write out the check."

"I'm sorry, wait. A check?" my dad said. The girl stopped at the harsh tone in his voice. He had put his hands on the counter and had started to step in front of me, pushing my mother aside and blocking me from the girl's view.

"Yes, sir. Is that okay?" Her accent seemed to thicken as she became more nervous in the presence of my dad. "Okay" sounded more like "O-Kai." And even though I felt sorry for her for having to deal with my dad, the girl's accent made me like her that much more. I could listen to her talk all day. My parents didn't speak with an accent, and neither did I. Only morons talked like that, my parents had told me.

And I knew they would never think a cute waitress in a country diner was worth their time. Or mine. Not for a second.

My dad was standing directly against the counter now. He was starting to raise his voice. "No," he was saying, "it's not okay to give my son a check. He's only twelve years old. He doesn't even have a bank account."

"Well, I'm sure the Hibernia across the street will cash it, sir," Heather Anne said, glancing down at me for a second with what looked like pity. "Let me just go get Mr. Ray, though, okay? He'll be able to tell you more about it than I can."

My dad shook his head as Heather Anne walked back into the kitchen. "Figures," he said, looking back at me. "You see, son? There are always strings attached to things like this. Every single time.

First, they want to write you a check. Next thing they're asking for your social security number to cash the damn thing. Then they have a record of everything you do. Big Brother, man. Never ceases to amaze me."

"Oh, come on, John," my mother said. "Just let him get his money. Do we have to make a moral issue out of everything?"

"This isn't about morals. I'm just trying to teach our son to be careful, Rebekah—to be aware of things."

"Well, maybe you can teach him later. Why does it have to be here?"

By now, Mr. Ray was coming out from the kitchen with Heather Anne following timidly behind him. My dad had apparently frightened her. What was even more frightening, though, was that I knew he hadn't even gotten started yet.

Mr. Ray was smiling and wiping his hands across his greasy apron. When he got to the counter, he reached out to shake my dad's hand, but he ignored the gesture. Mr. Ray frowned momentarily, then looked around behind my dad to where I was standing.

"So this must be the artist," he said, the smile reluctantly returning to his face as he looked at me, the expression creasing the tanned flesh at the corners of his eyes and mouth into a bunch of tiny lines—like a dozen small streams and rivers on some old, water-bent map. He looked kind, and I hated the fact that my parents were here with me. I wished I could've just come in by myself. "I'd like to shake your hand, young man."

"Please do me a favor," my dad said. "Don't inflate his ego." He moved back in front of me and pushed aside Mr. Ray's hand. "My son's drawings were rudimentary at best. When you tell him all that, then we have to go home and deal with him. Not you. So please don't patronize him."

"Do what now?"

My dad didn't waste time repeating himself. He just said, "Is there any way you can pay my son in cash? We really aren't interested in leaving a paper trail."

"Pardon me?"

"Well, in case you didn't realize, checks require signatures. Then these banks want your social security number to cash them. My son's a minor, and I'm really not interested in getting the federal government any more involved in our lives than they already are. After all, this whole damned contest is sponsored by the government—the public schools. Isn't it our country's First Lady who started this whole brainwashing scam about drugs in the first place? To distract kids from what's really happening in the world? I doubt it's a coincidence that her husband is an actor."

"John, please stop," my mother said. "This man doesn't want to hear this."

"Yeah," my dad said. "Ignorance is bliss, right?"

"I'm sorry, sir," Mr. Ray said, "but I'm not too sure I know what you're getting at here. Your son just won an award. You should be proud of him." Mr. Ray was looking at my dad as he said this, then he looked over at my mother. I had seen this look so many times before. It was a look of confusion mixed with anger and, at the bottom of that, a deep, deep sadness that came from seeing me—an innocent boy subjected to the whims of his willful and overly opinionated parents—being left with no choice but to tacitly go along with them.

"Proud?" my dad said. He laughed then, looking down at me as though I were a dog that just had an accident on the floor. "I don't think it's healthy to encourage children to feel pride over their earthly accomplishments. You and the people like you who run the public schools are just encouraging mediocrity, creating a flock of mindless sheep in the process, who'll grow up blind and ignorant to the ways in which this world is oppressing them. I say you're part of the problem, sir, if you're not part of the solution."

Mr. Ray didn't say anything for a good two or three seconds. Instead, he just stared at my dad, whose neck and face were now flushed the mottled red of anger and frustration. When Mr. Ray finally did speak, his words and tone seemed measured, greatly controlled, as if he were trying to keep himself from jumping over the counter and throttling my dad's neck. And I couldn't blame him if that is what he wanted to do. I'd often fantasized about doing that very thing myself.

"I'm sorry, sir," Mr. Ray finally said, "but I have to write you a check. It's for tax reasons. You see, I donate the prize money, then I get to write off—"

"Yeah, yeah," my dad interrupted. "I know how the government works. I think you have to remember that you're not talking to one of your corn-pone customers—someone who's standing here looking to be poisoned by your food. I'm an educated man, and I am well aware of what this is all about. Quid pro quo, right? Isn't that how it works? But whatever. Go ahead. Write your check. We'll be good little citizens and help everyone start up the massive paper trail on our son. A nice mountain of paper on his shoulders before he's even thirteen years old. That's what we'll leave behind for him when we die, right? God bless America." To my great horror and embarrassment, my dad actually sang these last three words. Loud. Anyone in the restaurant who hadn't been staring before was certainly staring at us now.

My dad turned to my mother. "And, Rebekah, what ever even possessed you to let him participate in this public school pyramid scheme, in the first place? Can you answer that for me?"

"John, it was just a drawing. I didn't even know he mailed it in. Come on, for God's sake."

"For God's sake," my dad repeated, laughing now. "For God's sake, huh? Is this all for the sake of God that we bow down to this man in his greasy little apron?"

My dad was raising his voice to the point where he was actually shouting. A couple that was sitting in a booth eating cheeseburgers and drinking milkshakes frowned at us. Heather Anne moved a step closer to Mr. Ray. She looked genuinely terrified.

"For God's sake," my dad said again, this time in a harsher, more matter-of-fact tone. "That's exactly why I'm here, Rebekah. This is my son. And I don't want to raise another slave to the government. I thought we agreed on this when we had him."

"We did, John, but we could really use this money right now, don't you think?"

We. And just then I knew that by saying this, my mother really meant "they," as in her and my dad. The money I won—against their wishes and without their support or encouragement—would now be used for the "greater good." A term they would most likely toss out at me later like a piece of wadded-up paper.

"I'm not going to sacrifice our principles," my dad said, pounding the counter with his fist to better-punctuate his message.

"Sir," Mr. Ray said calmly. "I'm going to have to ask you to leave now."

"See, John?" my mother said. "You are a complete embarrassment. Look at your son. He can't even show his face." She was pulling at my dad's shirtsleeve, trying to make him look at me. I stepped away.

Then my dad pulled back his arm from my mother's grip, and my mother screamed. Loud. As though my dad had punched her. Or stabbed her in the side with one of the forks from the counter. But of course, he hadn't. He had simply pulled his arm away and rested it against his leg. Still my mother screamed as loud as she possibly could, attracting a simultaneously frightened and deeply concerned glare from everyone in the restaurant.

A couple of men near the front who had been eating po-boys stood up from their table and looked at us. One of them placed his hand on a cracked leather holster that was attached to his belt, unsnapped it to reveal the handgun resting there. I don't think he was a cop, either. He was just another person reacting to my parents' bizarre behavior.

"It's all right, y'all," Mr. Ray said to them. "You can sit back down, fellas. These folks are on their way out right now." He looked at my parents. "Aren't y'all?"

"Come on, Eli," my dad said. "We don't need Big Brother's money anyway. What—just so he can tell us how to live our lives? I don't think so. Personally, I choose for us to remain free."

My dad turned around and started walking out of the restaurant. He looked proud of himself, a small grin on his face, his chest puffed out like a rooster's as he pushed open the door and walked outside. The rusted-out little bell above the door dinged as my dad walked under it. My mother followed him and I turned and followed her.

"Young man," Mr. Ray said as I was walking away. I turned around. "I'm sorry," he said. "That comic you drew really was good. Don't quit doing that, you hear? You really do have a knack for telling stories."

"Thanks," I whispered, hoping my parents wouldn't hear. I already knew I was in for a serious lecture when we got home, and any subtle alliance with this man—whom they would undoubtedly view as the enemy—would be met with more discussion and philosophical lecturing than I cared to hear. I just wanted it to all be over. So I turned back toward the open door where my mother and father were standing in a white rectangle of sunlight. Waiting.

4

Thankfully, by the time we got home, my parents had calmed down a bit after fighting for what seemed the whole ride back. I was sitting in the bed of my dad's pickup truck and my parents were both in the cab, but still I could hear them yelling and arguing, could see through the dirt-smeared window their arms flailing back and forth at one another as they most likely fought over who had been right and who had been wrong in the restaurant that afternoon.

Occasionally, the truck would swerve over the centerline as my dad let go of the steering wheel to push my mother away from him. Then he would right it too hard and the truck would lurch off the highway and onto the gravel shoulder, kicking up a cloud of brown dust and a spray of rocks behind it. I kept my head down and tried to hold on to the lip of the truck bed so I wouldn't slide around too much.

And the whole while I knew that somehow they would both manipulate this situation into being my fault. If I hadn't entered that contest, they'd say, none of this would have ever happened. If I hadn't been so determined to be part of a corrupt society, the government would leave us alone and we would all be happy right where we were. They'd say I was ungrateful for the life I had, for the opportunities they were giving me by teaching me to think for myself.

And I was right.

When we pulled up into our driveway, my parents climbed out of the cab, looked at me with anger-reddened faces, and told me to go inside. My mother, I could tell, had been crying.

My dad's previous anger from when we were in the restaurant had turned into disappointment now, it seemed—a disappointment that he wore on his face like one of those signs he used to make when he was younger, before I was born, and which he still kept scattered around the yard: pieces of moldy plywood with random Biblical verses painted across their cracked surfaces in large black letters, some of them leaning up against pine trees or the side of the tin shed in our backyard. Calling us out as sinners, exhorting us for our lack of faith. Our lack in general.

I walked into the house and sat down on the sofa and waited for my parents to come inside, waited for the lecture I knew was coming. When they walked up onto the porch, they were standing side by side and nearly touching. I had never once seen my parents hold hands or hug one another before, but I could tell by their body language that they had already formed an alliance against me—that they had joined together in their mutual anger and distrust of the outside world—and that all of this would now be my own sin for which I'd have to privately or perhaps even publicly atone. I waited.

"Son," my dad said, coming inside and sitting down in his wicker rocking chair next to the sofa, leaning back as far is it would let him go. "Your mother and I talked a good deal about what you've done today. The grief you've put upon this family."

He looked at me. Waited a moment in order to let his words have time to sink in.

My mother had gone into the kitchen to pour glasses of water for us to drink. I could hear the glasses slowly filling up and the ice tapping the sides of the glass; it was the only sound breaking the silence between what my dad had just said and what I knew he was about to finish with.

When my mother had the glasses ready, she came into the den and handed one to me, one to my dad. She kept the third one for herself, then sat down next to me on the sofa. Her eyes were still red-rimmed and swollen from crying and yelling at my dad on the way home.

"I want you to know that your mother and I are very disappointed that you disobeyed us," my dad continued.

"But y'all never said I couldn't—"

"Wait, Eli. Please don't interrupt me. You submitted that drawing to support a cause that you know your mother and I don't agree with. Don't you see how wrong that was?"

My dad didn't wait for my response. He kept on. "We could've just taken that check, sure, but then what? We would've had to cash it, give out your private information, have the school system down our throats again about you not being in school.

"Don't you realize they could send your mother and me to jail for that if they wanted to? It's called 'truancy,' Eli. Look it up.

"This world's a dangerous place, son," he continued, "and you have to be careful is all we're saying. Your mother and I are trying to protect you. Because we love you. Do you understand that?" He still didn't wait for me to answer. I kept my head down, looking at my shoes, moving the melting cubes of ice around in my glass with my finger. The condensation on the outsides of the glass made it slide in my hand. I wanted to just let it fall on the floor, watch it break into a million pieces. I wanted to walk away and never come back.

I looked over at my mother, who was staring at her glass of water, watching the tiny particles of dust—or whatever it was floating around in there—as though there was some message to be found in its movements. She didn't say anything either.

For a minute, the room was quiet, and no one spoke.

"Well, if no one has anything else to add," my dad finally said, getting up, "I have some work to do outside for Mr. Tally."

Then he looked over at me again. "Eli, I want you to go to your room and think about everything that happened today. And I would suggest praying about it. Asking the Lord for forgiveness."

"Yes, sir," I said.

I got up, looked at my mother, who seemed to be dozing now where she was sitting on the sofa, her glass of water tilted slightly in her hand, a soft breath whispering out of her half-opened mouth like a cat purring. After her and my dad fought like that, she would often be exhausted, would go to her room and sleep for the rest of the day. I didn't say anything to her.

Instead, I went to my room, where I sat by myself until it was nearly dark outside. I hadn't eaten all day, but I wasn't about to go out there to face my parents again. Instead. I had spent the afternoon and that early part of evening thumbing through some of the books I had lying around on my floor, trying to teach myself, as my parents had expected me to do—although it was with no direction or order. I just read haphazardly, scanned through pictures in the incomplete encyclopedia set I had. Looked up words in the dictionary. Manacle. Fetter. Trammel.

At one point, as dusk was spreading across the sky like a warm sheet being tossed over a mattress, I heard my mother finally get up from the sofa where she had been napping, leave the den, and then go to her room. I could hear her bare feet brushing against the wood floor, some of the loose planks creaking lightly under her wispy frame like someone's fingers brushing against the keys of a piano, the kind of music my mother often listened to while she was in the kitchen doing dishes or some other menial task like cooking, the little window above the sink open and whisking the tiny curtain over it back and forth as the hot dishwater breathed thick tendrils of steam into my mother's sad, sad face.

A few minutes later, I heard her in her room fooling around with her records. She finally put on The Beatles's White Album. I wasn't allowed a record player or a radio in my room, and even if I had been, I think I would've preferred the silence. Sometimes I hated my mother's music. Something about it made me worry about her. My dad didn't approve of the secular music my mother listened to either, but she was stubborn when it came to her records. She refused to give up her collection, which contained albums by Cat Stevens, Joni Mitchell, Bob Dylan. All of these songs made me terribly sad, though, even more disconnected from my mother's internal world.

But on that day, as John Lennon sang "Dear Prudence," a song about a girl who herself rarely left her room, I could completely relate to the feeling he was singing about. And although the subject of the song's lyrics had chosen to stay inside to meditate or pray or whatever it was that kept her there, I couldn't help but think about how the world outside was moving along without me as I sat stuck in my bedroom, the sun rising and falling, the birds singing, the children playing. Every day the same. And yet, here I was in my room. Alone. All as Lennon implored that I just open my eyes and look around. If only it were that easy.

5

Much later, after hours of sitting in my bed and staring at the wall, flipping through the moldy-smelling pages of my books, and trying not to think about the hunger pains in my stomach, I finally looked outside my window and could see the moon hanging high up in the sky as though it were one of God's own cast-off fingernail clippings. It glowed a yellow-white in the navy, star-spackled sea around it. Everything was quiet. I had heard my dad come inside from the barn a little while earlier, go into the kitchen, and then fix himself something to eat. Then I heard him go back out onto the front porch, where I could hear the sound of his rocking chair creaking against the porch slats.

My mother was still in her room, but she had turned off her music by then. I imagined she was probably lying in her bed, sleeping. It was only about seven o'clock or so, but my mother slept a lot—especially if she was depressed or had taken too many of those pills she was always swallowing, which she was doing more and more of lately, it seemed. And maybe that's why she had laughed at my comic strip—because if she had been offered a handful of pills like that, maybe she would have just happily accepted them.

When her own mother had died a couple of years ago, both my parents went to her house to help clean it out. Somehow my mother ended up with all these translucent brown bottles of pain pills and sedatives. My parents said it was important to keep those around in case "something happened," by which I knew they meant the end of the world. This was something else they were both obsessed with and trying to prepare me for. (They buried money in metal boxes in the back yard, kept gas masks under the kitchen sink, barrels of wheat and rice in the shed outside—all in preparation for what they saw as the inevitable collapse of an already-fallen world.) Over the past few months, however, I had noticed my mother taking these pills herself. Sometimes more than twice in a given day.

After a while, I finally decided to just try to fall asleep myself. There was just nothing else to do. I had thought a little about climbing out the window and walking around in the pasture some until it got late and I was tired, but I didn't want to risk my dad coming into my room to find me missing. He would likely stir up my mother in the process, and everything would descend back into chaos. And of course I would be to blame again.

So I took off my shoes and climbed into bed. But as I pulled the sheets down, I heard my dad coming back inside from where he had been sitting on the porch. The screen door smacked shut behind him and then I heard his heavy footsteps coming down the hall toward my room. He opened the door without knocking.

"Eli?" he said. "Are you still awake?"

"Yes, sir," I said.

"Good. You know, I've been thinking a lot about what happened today. Praying about it, in fact. And I think I owe you an apology of sorts."

I didn't say anything, just kept my eyes cast down toward my feet.

"This is not to say that what you did was okay," he said. "I don't want you to get that impression. Not at all. But what I am trying to tell you is that I believe God has had a hand in all of this, as He does with all of our earthly matters. Sometimes it just takes us a while to see it."

"Yes, sir," I said.

"I think I see now what it is that God wants, Eli. He wants me to teach you about the world, what exactly it is your mother and I are trying to protect you from. That way you'll know what to run from when it comes. And trust me, young man, it is coming. Something's definitely coming over the horizon. In Revelation it says, 'I looked, and behold a pale horse: and his name that sat on him was Death, and Hell followed with him.' This is what's coming, Eli. And it is our duty, as your parents, to show it to you."

I looked at my dad, who was standing in the doorway, blocking out what little light was leaking in from the hall. I was surprised to see that he was actually smiling. It wasn't quite an expression of joy, though; his smile had the look of something much more sinister. It's hard to put my finger on, but I can say this much: my dad had told my mother and me once that he was actually looking forward to the Apocalypse. He had said he wasn't afraid of it, that he knew where he would go when the world went up in flames. "I'm actually excited about it," he had said that day. "We'll finally get to go home to our Lord."

"You're ill," my mother had told him coldly.

I'll never forget that.

Anyway, that's the same smile my dad had on his face just then, when he finally said, "I'm going to take you to that fair tonight after all, Eli." In his mind, I think, he was going to give me a glimpse of the end of the world, of sin in its purest form; and that I would finally see what it was he was trying to protect me from. Then I'd come running into the fold. He seemed elated by the idea. He was going to teach me something that no school ever could.

I didn't even care what his reasons were, though. All I cared about was the fact that we were getting out of the house. I jumped up from my bed.

"What? Really?" I said.

"Well, I want you to see that secular entertainment is not all it's cracked up to be."

He could say whatever he wanted to about why we were going, it didn't matter. I just wanted to be doing something that normal people did, and I didn't want him to have another second to reconsider.

As I was putting my shoes back on over my gray socks, he droned on: "And while, yes," he was saying, "it's true that I am leading you into temptation, the idea is to ultimately deliver you from evil."

"Okay," I said. I was already at the foot of my bed, waiting to go.

"Go get your mother then," he said.

"Yes, sir." I almost sprinted down the narrow hallway to wake her.

"Mom!" I called out, knocking on her door two times and then opening it before she could say anything. I flicked on the light and she sat up in her bed quickly, as though I had startled her.

She looked dazed. Disheveled. Her eyes were puffy underneath and bloodshot, and her hair was sticking up in the back from where it had been smashed into her pillow. "Eli?" she said. "Wh—what's wrong?"

"Nothing," I said. "Dad said we can go to the fair."

"What? He did?"

"Yeah," I said. "Come on. Get dressed. Before he changes his mind."

But my mother hardly moved. Instead, she sat staring at me as though I were an apparition. She reached slowly over and picked up her glass of water from the nightstand. Sipped from it. Licked her dry lips. Stared again at the particles floating around in the glass. It was as though she were moving through spiderwebs, or walls pulled taut with gauze.

"Eli, I don't know if I want to go with y'all. I'm too tired," she finally said, speaking slowly and slurring her words. "Your father really wants to do this?"

"Yes, he said so. Can me and him just go then?" I didn't want to leave my mother home alone like that, I really didn't, but this was my only chance to get out of that house. I knew I had to take it or just be stuck there.

"I don't care, Eli. Y'all can just go," she said.

"Okay, Mom. Are you sure?" I said.

"Yeah, go."

"Okay, Mom. Bye." I felt bad for being so abrupt with her, but I figured she'd probably just go back to sleep anyway; she might not even remember me coming into her room, only to wake up later thinking she had dreamed it all.

"Be careful," she was saying as I gently pulled the door shut against its frame. Then I walked down the hall and into the den where my dad was waiting.

"Where's your mother?" he said.

"She said she's too tired, but that she didn't care if me and you just went."

"You and I," he corrected.

"You and I," I said.

He smiled again. "Well, let's go then."

I knew there must have still been some tension between my parents from earlier, especially since my dad didn't go in to check on my mother or ask if she was sure she didn't want to go. He was probably happy she decided to stay home. My parents could sometimes be reasonable enough to know they shouldn't be around each other. Maybe this was one of those times.

We walked outside and got into the truck. My dad started the engine and I watched as the headlights washed over the tall grass in our yard, the overgrown bushes and trees. The truck slouched over the craters in our dirt-and-gravel driveway and, as we pulled out, I looked over at Mr. Tally's house across the field and could see his silhouette framed in the yellow porch light. He was probably wondering where we were going at this hour, especially since my parents rarely left the house after dusk, if at all. Maybe I would tell him about it next time I talked to him. I doubted he'd even believe me. I couldn't even believe it was happening myself.

6

The drive from Angie to Franklinton takes about forty minutes and we saw only about three cars on the road until we got into town. My dad didn't say much, but instead kept the radio tuned to a gospel station where the announcer was talking about End Times and where the occasional caller would call in and yell about the signs all around us—could we not see them with our own eyes, he said—that were indeed preceding the fiery demise of the human race.

"They're everywhere," the crackling voice screamed through the old speakers near my legs. "Even in nature is signs. It don't take an idiot to see 'em."

I tried to ignore this as we drove—I'd heard enough of it at home every day—thinking about the fair instead and looking at the crystal-clear water in the gravel pits on either side of the highway. The sliver of moon overhead was reflected in the corrugated surface of the water. The ponds themselves looked to be composed of tiny, rippling mirrors embedded in the sand and the rocks. It was beautiful, and it was hard to imagine God really wanting to destroy all of this.

I could only imagine what the fair would be like as I looked into those shiny pools of water as my dad drove down the lonely highway, the little yellow ticks in the middle of the road seeming to move toward us as though we were on a conveyor belt instead of actually driving.

My mother had a book about old fairs and circuses during the early twentieth century, and I remembered the black-and-white and sepia-toned images of striped canvas tents and tiny men lifting large barbells over their heads, the women with beards that grew to the middle of their chests. This is what I was imagining in the hot cab of my dad's truck that night.

In my head I saw lots of lights and shiny spinning rides, could smell cotton candy and caramel and popcorn, horses and the sweet smell of dusty hay and grass. I heard calliopes playing and men calling out to the crowds as they milled slowly past the booths, which were strung together with orange electrical cords, like spiderwebs, each one dotted with large white light bulbs burning a hazy circle of light onto the ground. It was dizzying just to think about.

I was buried in these thoughts when I looked up and realized that my dad was slowing down the truck. We had already crossed through town, passing under the blinking yellow caution lights, all of which I had hardly noticed, and now suddenly we were there. The Washington Parish Fairgrounds. "The belly of the beast," my dad said as he engaged the parking brake and shut off the engine. "You ready?"

"Yes," I said, smiling slightly, trying to knead the solemnness out of this moment, which I was still hoping would be fun.

My dad had parked in the grass next to a ditch choked with weeds, but the truck was at a slanted angle so that when I opened my door to get out, the edge of it got caught in the muddy ground. I climbed out of the cab and stepped over the ditch to try to shut the door, but couldn't get it out of the mud. The weeds brushed up against the interior of the truck like fingers grabbing for purchase at the edge of a rocky cliff.

"Dad," I said. "My door's stuck. I can't get it shut."

My dad stood by his own opened door and he was looking through the still-lit cab at what I had done. He sucked his teeth and shook his head, mumbled something under his breath. I couldn't hear what he said, but it sounded like a curse word, a rare utterance for him. Then he slammed his door. I couldn't tell if he closed it that way out of anger or if it was simply the angle of the truck that caused the door to shut with more force than it normally would have. I was very tense and paranoid; I knew that I was over-thinking everything, but I just didn't want to screw this up. Any moment he could change his mind and take me back home.

Because even though we were here, I still felt as though this were a tenuous event—as though I were walking on a tightrope and could, at any second, fall off. My dad had little patience, and something like this could be just enough to make him turn back. I pushed on the door again, trying to close it. But still it barely moved.

My dad came around from the driver's side of the truck to where I was standing. He crossed over the ditch and told me to move. Then he tried to close the door himself. Nothing. A clump of muddy grass was caught on the corner of the door and he couldn't get it shut either.

"Son of a bitch," he said. This time he didn't try to hide the fact that he was cursing. I figured I had blown my chance now for sure.

"Sorry," I said.

"Look, just watch out, okay? I'm going to have to pull up a little bit so you can get that door shut."

"Okay," I said.

Then he walked back around the front of the truck, pulled his keys from his pocket, unlocked his door, and climbed back inside the cab. I heard the truck grumble back to life as he started it, then watched as he put it in gear and pulled up about six inches, enough to free the door from its place in the mud. I walked up to it and pushed it shut, hoping it wouldn't give him enough time to change his mind, to call me back into the cab to leave.

But thankfully he didn't. Instead, he turned off the engine and climbed out of the cab, slammed his door again, and started walking along the side of the road toward the entrance to the fairgrounds.

"Come on," he said. I could tell he was angry, but at least we weren't leaving.

I followed him. The last thing I heard as we walked away was the engine ticking as it cooled, and then I was enveloped by the sounds of the fair. It was everything—and more—that I had imagined on the drive over there. The lights. The smells. The music. The laughter. The sound of the rides going up and down and around on their metal tracks, the people riding them screaming with what could have been delight, or fear. Or both. It was perfect.

Now my dad was trying to tell me something about how it was God's design that my door got stuck like that. How God was trying to keep us from entering this den of sin and evil and depravity, and how by disobeying Him like this, something terrible was likely to happen. But still we pressed on.

I just tried to block out what he was telling me. It was such a contradiction to what he had been saying earlier when he stood in the doorway to my room, smiling at me. He had told me then that it was God's will that we come here. Now it was the opposite. But that's how he was. I could never be certain—and to this day am still unsure about it—if my dad was perpetually confused himself or if he just liked to confuse me. My strategy was just to ignore him as best I could, to simply take in all that was around me instead. To make my own opinions.

"We're only going to stay for a few minutes," he was saying.

"We'll go find your drawing in the exhibits section—isn't that what they said in the letter?—then maybe we can look at the animals, and that's it. No rides or anything like that. Understood?"

"Yes, sir," I said.

As we neared the entrance to the fairgrounds, a group of teenagers passed us, their black T-shirts embossed with the cracked logos of bands like Metallica, Megadeth, Iron Maiden, Guns N' Roses, and Ozzy Osbourne (I recognized these logos since my parents seemed to spend a great deal of their time protesting this kind of music, telling me how evil it was) barely visible in the dark; the orange glow of their cigarettes briefly illuminated each of their pale, acne-ridden faces as they walked by.

One of them, a boy with dark hair that was shaved on the sides but was long in the back and cascaded down his shoulders like a muddy waterfall, stopped in front of my dad and pretended to take a picture of him with his yellow fingers. The boy held both of his hands together as if he were holding a camera and then he pressed down his index finger and clicked his tongue against his teeth to make the appropriate sound effect.

"Snap!" he said.

The other kids started laughing and they moved on, a cloud of gray smoke rising up from their group as though it were exhaust coming out of a passing eighteen-wheeler. I tried not to stare at them as they disappeared into the darkness. I had no idea what prompted that boy to do that, but I could tell my dad was greatly disturbed by it as he turned to watch them go. He just shook his head solemnly.

Then he faced forward again, still shaking his head from side to side. "See?" he said. "That's exactly what your mother and I have been telling you about. Exactly the kinds of kids we don't want you associating with. That's what our public school systems are mass-producing these days: a bunch of drug-addicted psychopaths. And our tax dollars are paying for it all. Wonderful, isn't it?"

I didn't say anything. It was hard for me to have an opinion about any of these things my parents went on and on about when, in fact, there was a secret part of me that wished I could be one of those kids. Was that really a terrible thing? To have fun? And who said they were doing drugs just because they listened to heavy metal and smoked cigarettes? So what, I thought.

The lights from the fairgrounds were brighter now as we walked between the enormous brick columns that created the wide entry leading onto the midway. This was a free fair so we didn't have to pay to get in. Otherwise, I know my dad would've never taken me.

Those brick columns flanking the entrance must have been twenty feet high, and they were connected at the top with a long wooden sign that said "Washington Parish Fair." On top of that were about two dozen red, yellow, and green flags drooping down from their metal poles. They were deathly still as we walked beneath them.

I knew my dad was counting all of these things as Signs. Tallying them up in his head for later: the group of teenagers, the stuck door, even these seemingly innocuous flags. All Signs that we were disobeying God's will.

But I was too nervous, excited now that we were finally here, to think about all of that. There were so many people walking around on the dust-and-hay covered midway. Hundreds and hundreds of them swelling and flowing like an outgoing tide.

The sounds and smells were just as I had imagined too. In fact, they were even better: cotton candy, horses, popcorn, frying grease, cigarette smoke. My heart was a small bird in my chest. It was hard for me to take everything in.

"Stay close to me," my dad was saying. "Lots of scam artists here," he said. "And remember. We don't have any money."

"Okay," I said.

I wondered what my mother would think if she were here with us. If, like me, she would notice the things that brought so many people out of their lonely lives to come here and be together like this. Even if it was only for just one night. To me, this was all magic.

But regardless of how my mother might have felt, I know my dad wouldn't have seen it that way as we walked through the milieu of sweaty, anxious, and loud people. He would have been quietly judging all of them for their sinful ways, their moral degradation.

I knew that in his mind he was preparing his sermon for when we got home later. But I wasn't worried about it now. I was determined to enjoy this evening as best I could.

As we walked down the midway toward the exhibits to see some of the cows from Mr. Tally's farm (my dad had mentioned this as we were walking, as if to further justify his reason for taking me here), as well as to look at my "Just Say No" comic, which was supposed to be on display back there too, we were stopped by a wall of onlookers who were piled up in front of one of the many wooden booths that flanked the midway. There were enough people standing there in a loose, rather disorganized semicircle that it prevented anyone from getting past them on either side.

We stopped, and our eyes followed the collective stares to the front of the booth where a man was lying on the ground in the dirt and tossing darts at a corkboard with his bare feet. The man on the ground had no arms; I looked on in awe as one after another, these little plastic-and-metal darts arced up from where this man lay in the dirt and then made their way to the corkboard behind the barker who was manning the booth. He was a grizzled-looking man, probably about my dad's age, and even he seemed surprised by what he was bearing witness to.

When one of the darts finally hit a balloon that was dangling from the corkboard and the barker handed a large stuffed animal to a woman who appeared to be the armless man's girlfriend, the crowd started to disperse and my dad bent down and spoke into my ear.

"This is all a set up," he said. "It's a satanic spectacle. The worst kind of entertainment imaginable. Can you believe that? Someone with no arms? This is a freak show, Eli. Like that Hieronymus Bosch painting. Remember that awful thing you saw in the encyclopedia that time?"

I didn't say anything as my dad started to turn back toward the entrance, as though we were going to leave. I just stood there, looking at the man behind the booth and thinking about that painting: the twisted figures doing things that made my face turn red and feel hot when I remembered it. And I felt a strange sort of guilt just knowing I had looked upon it. Maybe that's what I was supposed to feel now at the fair, but for some reason I didn't. I was glad for that at least.

Then the carnival barker who had given over the stuffed animal caught me looking at him and called us over.

"Come on, young man," he said. "Check out the prizes here. There's something for everyone. And not just stuffed animals. Everyone's a winner tonight! Come give it a try. One dollar a dart. Gimme five dollars and you get six tries. That's one for free if your math ain't too good!"

"No, Eli," my dad was saying into my ear. "Remember what I told you."

He started to nudge me away from the booth but the barker was still yelling at us. "Don't run off!" he said. "Hey! You look like a good kid. So I'll tell you what: I'll give you one try for free. You hit a balloon, you get a prize. You miss, what did you lose? Nothing! Just the two seconds it took you to walk over here, that's all! You can't beat those odds, gentlemen! Any prize you want."

I don't know what came over me then, but I pulled away from my dad and went up to the man in the booth and looked over his prizes. In a glass case behind where all the darts were lined up was a small box with a little boot knife in it. There was a picture of it on the outside of the box: the knife had a wooden hilt and a double-edged blade and came with a little leather case to slide the knife into when you weren't using it. Something told me I had to have that knife.

"See something you like, young man?"

"That knife," I said softly, "I like that knife." My voice was coming from my mouth like it usually did, but it sounded different to me. Separate.

"That there's what they call a Bowie knife," he said. "And I'll tell you what, bub. I'll give you one try for free—like I said—and if you hit one of these here balloons and pop it, that knife's yours. Have you ever thrown a dart before?"

"No, sir," I said. "I've never even been to a fair before."

"What?" the man said, sounding genuinely surprised. Most of

what he said had seemed rehearsed, but his reaction to my never having been to a fair, I could tell, was genuine. He really was shocked. It was as though, from his perspective, all kids experienced this sort of thing, and without question too—like it was a rite of passage or something. "Is that your dad back there?" he said.

"Yes, sir."

The barker looked back at my dad, who was still standing about fifteen feet behind me, his arms crossed over his chest, his lips shut tightly and folded into a straight line. He looked as angry as he probably felt for my disobeying him. I would just have to worry about that later.

The barker smiled and waved at him. He didn't wave back. "Come on, Dad," the barker said. "Loosen up! Your boy's going to have some fun! And I have a strong feeling he's going to walk away from here a winner tonight. Or my name's not Harlow Cagwin!"

My dad was silent, still. A couple of people walked past him, bumped against his shoulder on their way down the muddy lane, but he didn't move to let them pass easily.

"Your old man's a tough customer," the barker—Mr. Cagwin—said.

"He thinks this place is wicked," I said, still surprised at my candor with this strange man. But there was an openness about him that I couldn't explain. Or maybe something had come open inside of me: just being here like this, with my dad, a witness to such a strange experience.

"Well, he might be right about that, son, but you only live once, as the saying goes. Might as well enjoy the ride before it stops."

I didn't know what to say to this man, so I just looked down at the row of darts, then at that knife in the glass case. It sat there as if it were watching me.

I picked up one of the darts and held it between my fingers, then turned it around to feel the heft of it in my hand.

Mr. Cagwin stepped out of the way, lifted the nub of cigarette he had been holding between his fingers up to his lips, then inhaled deeply. The end glowed bright orange under the dull yellow light bulbs, which were draped from one of the wooden beams above his head like apples hanging from a tree branch. They reminded me of the apples my parents told me about in Genesis. All that poisonous knowledge, just waiting to be picked and eaten. And here I was, about to partake in a different kind of forbidden fruit. I grasped the dart.

Everything slowed down, the sounds and smells around me disintegrated. My dad's presence, too, became nonexistent. It was just me, that dart, and this strange man Harlow, standing between it all like some weird gatekeeper.

I knew that my dad would never pay for me to get another try, so I had to pop one of those balloons now. I rolled the dart around between my thumb and middle finger a couple more times, trying to get a better sense of its weight in my hand.

After looking at the dart and holding it between my fingers for a minute, feeling the cold metal against the hard callouses on my skin, I stepped back and away from the table, pulling my arm up over my shoulder, as though I were about to toss a football. I knew that getting the distance on it wouldn't be a problem, nor would throwing the dart hard enough to pop one of the balloons. It was really just a matter of getting it to land in just the right spot, and at just the right angle.

I looked at this man Cagwin, who was still watching me carefully, smoking his cigarette with one of his legs propped against a two by four that made up the back frame of his booth. Then I looked at the corkboard again and the balloons that were scattered across it. I could see the ones that had already been popped hanging from nails or thumbtacks, little pieces of rubber drooping down like strips of dried, colorful meat in a smokehouse, all the rest of the holes pocked across the board's surface like so many stars in the sky.

I focused my eyes on a yellow balloon that seemed to be the most inflated, figuring I had the best chance of popping one that had more air inside of it. I honed in my vision on that balloon, as though it were the only object that existed—that and the dart I was about to throw at it.

Then I flung my arm forward and let the dart go, watching it arc slightly before it went straight for my intended target. Before it even hit the balloon, I knew that I had thrown perfectly. I could feel it in my gut, just knew it was going to hit. The only question was whether or not the balloon would actually pop.

But then I heard it.

The sharp point met with the balloon's skin and it burst instantaneously. And just as suddenly, the rest of the world came back into focus: I could hear the people my dad had held up by not moving out of their way standing behind me. They were clapping and cheering. I could once again see Cagwin, now flicking his cigarette out of his booth, where it landed in the dirt, orange sparks following behind it and slowly falling to the ground like burning flecks of snow. The music and the noise from the rides came back too. It was as though I had been in a foggy, soundless tunnel and was now emerging from the other end as it opened back up onto the world.

Cagwin was walking over to the corkboard and pulling out the dart as I made my way back toward him. I watched as he took a key from his shirt pocket and opened the little sliding glass door on the case that held the knife and a few other random items that I hadn't even noticed until then: a couple of lucky rabbit's feet, some fake dog tags that you could have engraved with your name if you wanted, some rock band posters in glass frames. But I didn't care about those things. I only wanted that knife.

Cagwin picked up the box and handed it over to me. "Good job, boy," he said, smiling. And what was odd was that he looked genuinely happy, as though he could sense how much this meant to me. "You see? I told you it was your lucky day," he said.

Then he looked up and out at the rest of the crowd, seeming to avoid looking in the direction where I imagined my dad was still standing. "See, folks, everyone's a winner here. Come try your luck. Three dollars, three darts. Five bucks gets you six." His voice trailed off and started to sound like a cassette tape that had just been unpaused, the music from it blending back into a sea of ambient noise.

I turned to where my dad had been standing, saw that he had already walked away and was heading toward the exhibits. I was shocked that he wasn't leaving the fair altogether after what had just happened. And even though I knew that I would be in trouble later, I still followed him. I had no choice. But first I opened the box and took out the knife, which was resting in its leather sleeve.

I pulled it from its sheath and looked at it, turned it over in my hand. It was mine. Really mine. The light from overhead reflected on the smooth blade as I slid it back in its case. Then I clipped it to my belt and tossed the empty box in a trash barrel that was heaped over with empty Coke cans and half-eaten corn dogs resting in soggy plates made of red-and-white checkered cardboard, ketchup and mustard staining their grease-sodden sides like some bizarre murder scene.

I followed my dad. Somehow I felt different with the knife clipped to my belt. I still couldn't believe it: It was something that was mine, something I had gotten on my own, and I was proud of it. My parents had always told me that pride was a sin, and I knew they were probably right but, this time, I thought that maybe it wasn't so bad. I wasn't necessarily proud of myself, but just proud of what the knife represented: something new and in defiance of my parents. I figured they'd come around eventually. Maybe my dad would even find a reason to use the knife himself one day. Maybe he'd even thank me for winning it.

7

When I finally made it through the midway to where the exhibits were set up, I could no longer see my dad. There were so many people milling around that, instead of panicking, I decided to look for my comic strip, which was supposed to be displayed on one of the boards next to the other schools' exhibits. I thought that my dad may even be standing in front of it, waiting for me to get there. But I was wrong. When I finally found my drawing, my dad was nowhere to be seen. I don't know if he even came in there to look at it or not, but still I stood there for a minute and read over my story for the first time since I had placed it in the return envelope and mailed it off.

Again that feeling of pride started to well up inside of me, and I tried to push it down, but something about seeing my own creation hanging in what I thought was a prominent place next to other kids' work made me feel good about myself. Was that such a bad thing? I knew my parents would think so. After all, neither one of them were even here to enjoy this moment with me. I didn't care. That was my time, my moment to feel a part of the world and to be okay with myself.

I looked at the other displays. Most of them were from kids who actually went to area schools, and I thought it must have said something about my ability as an artist and a storyteller that my piece had won the contest, even though I was home-schooled. Maybe it was a testament, after all, to my parents' abilities as teachers. Maybe I had underestimated them, had been too critical of their unorthodox methods. Maybe I just needed to have more faith. I knew that's what they would probably tell me anyway.

"Are one of these yours?" a voice leaned in from beside me. I had been so wrapped up in looking at all the drawings and by what I was thinking that I literally jumped at the sound of it.

"I'm sorry," the voice said. "I didn't mean to scare you."

"That's okay," I said, looking over at the woman who was standing next to me. She was dressed very formally for a place like this, I thought, and she was much older than most people here. I wondered if she was a teacher, or maybe somebody's grandmother. "I was just daydreaming," I said.

"Well, there's nothing wrong with that. I think kids need to have dreams."

I didn't say anything, but immediately thought this woman was odd. Something about her seemed very out of place here.

"So, are you the artist responsible for any one of these?" she said.

"Yes, ma'am. I drew that one right there." I pointed to my comic strip, and the woman looked at it, then down at the blue ribbon that was stapled right next to it.

"Wow, first place," she said. "That's wonderful. Congratulations."

"Thanks."

"Are you here alone?"

"No, ma'am," I said. "my dad's here too. We just got separated. I'm actually about to go see if I can find him right now."

"Well, I'm glad to meet you," she said, squinting at the index card next to my drawing and reading my name from it, "Eli." Then she stepped back and looked at me, as if surprised a name like that would belong to a boy like me.

"That's a beautiful name," she said. "Do you know that it means 'my God' in Hebrew?"

"No, ma'am."

"Well, your parents must have thought quite highly of you to name you that. Perhaps they expect big things from you. Hopefully, you won't disappoint them."

"I won't," I said.

She smiled the way adults do when children say anything that's even remotely profound, even if it's not meant to sound that way. I hadn't wanted to impress her. I just wanted to get out of there and find my dad.

I started to walk away, feeling even stranger in this woman's presence than I had before. It was something about the way she spoke. No one around here talked like she did. Used words like "perhaps" or knew the Hebrew meanings of people's names. She sounded like someone from a big city or something, like someone who had gone to college.

Before I could get away, though, she said something else. "I see here on the placard that you're home-schooled, Eli." Placard. Another one of those big-city, college words.

"Yes, ma'am."

"You know the church I belong to has a home-schooler's group? They meet twice a week. I don't recall ever seeing you there. Maybe you'd like to tell your parents about it? See if they'd take you?"

"Sure," I said, having no intentions of telling them anything, as it would require an explanation of how I met this person. If I told them, I would have to confess that I was looking at my own artwork on display, which took pride. A sin. That particular floodgate would remain shut. I just wanted this strange woman to leave me alone.

"Great," she said. "Would you mind if I gave you something?"

I didn't say anything, but the woman reached into her tiny purse, which I hadn't even noticed until then. It hung stiffly at her side, just between where her elbow pressed into her ribcage. The purse was black and cylindrical in shape. It looked like a miniature cannon. She unsnapped the gold clasp and pulled out a handful of tracts. Or maybe they were brochures. I couldn't tell which at first. But I had seen these sorts of things before at other churches my parents had brought me to.

Then she handed me one and I took it, looked at the colorful wording and large, exclamatory fonts and text. Beneath where it said "Light of His Way: The Only **Way** to Eternal Salvation!" in soft blue lettering was a picture of a man with his arms outspread and his slightly smiling face looking skyward. His long hair and thick brown beard reminded me of a folk singer on the cover of one of my mother's records.

Beneath his gauzy-looking picture were the words, "unless one is *born again* he cannot see the kingdom of **God**.—Peter 3:3." Then in a slightly smaller font below that, but in yellow: "Receive your *Salvation*! Sundays @ 10AM"

I folded the tract and put it in my back pocket. "Thanks," I said.

"Now be sure you give that to your parents, Eli."

"I will."

"I really do have a feeling that this was not a chance encounter, young man. God's hand is upon us this evening. I want you to remember that," she said.

"Okay," I said. "I will."

I started to walk away, not wanting to look back, but like Lot's wife, I couldn't help myself. When I turned, this woman who hadn't even told me her own name was leaning over and removing the index card next to my drawing and placing it in her little pillbox purse with the biblical tracts she kept in there.

The card had my parents' and my names on it, first and last. The other cards had the kids' school listed on it, but since my parents were essentially my "school," their names were there instead. And although our phone number (we didn't even have a phone) and exact address weren't listed, it did say the name of the town where we lived: "Angie, LA," which was such a small place we wouldn't be hard at all to locate if someone really wanted to find us. I wondered why someone like that woman would even be interested in us anyway.

As I walked out of the exhibit, I turned again to see her moving slowly along the aisles as if she were in a fancy art museum. She really did look out of place there, what with the dirt-and-hay covered ground, her nice shoes powdered with brown dust from walking in it, her nice clothes. I wondered who she was as I walked back out into the midway, looking again for my dad, who by now had seemed to completely disappear.

8

When I finally found him, he was sitting among a crowd of people on a set of metal bleachers. The bleachers rose up in front of a large covered arena where cowboys were roping cattle, barrel racing, and bull riding.

The arena was flooded with light, country music blaring from tinny-sounding speakers, the announcer's voice breaking in occasionally to tell the audience the cowboy's name and the name of the bull he was attempting to ride. It was a cacophony of sound, which rode the swell of the crowd noise, becoming a sea of strange music.

Despite the fair lasting only a few days each October, the arena seemed to be a permanent fixture of the fairgrounds. There were large wooden pylons holding up a corrugated tin roof, two by fours and two by sixes ribbed overhead and veined with orange extension cords and strands of lights and bullhorns and other small speakers for music, or otherwise to project the announcer's voice across the arena.

On all sides were silver-colored, metal bleachers, which were littered with half-empty boxes of popcorn, plastic cups with bent straws protruding from their tops, wooden sticks with the crispy remains of the corn dogs that had once been impaled on them, all blanketed by the mud and clay from the boots of the people who sat there.

The bleachers rose up to just under the rafters so that sitting on the top row, you could almost touch the tin roof overhead and see the pigeons that nested there in the dark spaces, the beds of straw and shredded napkins visible among their spackled droppings.

Occasionally, the crowd would stand and cheer in unison as the cowboys were thrown from the bulls and scrambled up to their feet to run to the green metal gate that surrounded the arena, the bull running behind them, kicking up its legs wildly and flinging its head at the dirt, the stubs of horns protruding from it like broken branches on a wind-battered tree. Everything about this spectacle was wild and terrifying and exciting to me as I stood there looking up at my dad, who was almost camouflaged by the raging crowd around him.

In the middle of the dusty arena—and between the bull rides, which lasted only a few seconds each—would occasionally appear a clown, dancing under the stage lights and kicking up dust like one of the horses or bulls that had just gone back into the metal chutes and which corralled the animals into the holding area underneath the bleachers. You could hear them kicking and bucking against the metal gates and the cowboys talking to them.

"Come on, boy," they'd say, as if soothing a child. "Hold still now."

One of these rodeo clowns was standing in the middle of the arena when I first came in and saw my dad, who himself was sitting alone and looking down disapprovingly at what was taking place before him. The clown was dressed in a colorful red, yellow, and green shirt with large red pom-poms for buttons. His red curly wig puffed out from his head and almost belied his overly tanned and grizzled face, his bloodshot eyes, his cracked or missing teeth.

Even with the splotchy white face paint and the red circles on his cheeks, this clown looked more like a convict in disguise. Someone who would eat children—he reminded me of a Stephen King book I had once seen my mother looking at while we were in the library. I remember walking up to her and seeing the cover: half a clown's face protruding from a sewer drain, its hand a black dragon's claw covered with green misty clouds. As soon as I had walked up to her, she had put the book back on the shelf and acted as though she had been looking at something else. She later tried to explain to me that that book wasn't "literature." That it was trash reading for trashy people.

When I asked her why she had been looking at it then, she had just told me it was because in order to fight the enemy, you had to know your enemy.

As I looked back out onto the dusty arena, which was being bathed in white fluorescent light and the twang of country music, this rodeo clown was dancing around madly, kicking up spurts of dust, his over-sized jeans barely covering his large red shoes, which under the light and the sheen of brown dust and clay that covered them, appeared to be painted the color of blood.

In the distance, and just beside the metal gate where one of the cowboys had just climbed up to safety, there stood a fuming bull. His nostrils were flared wide and blowing up clouds of dust. The streaks of sweat in his dusty hide became rivulets running down his sides and face. He looked like one of those bison that had been drawn on a cave wall with globs of ocher, streaks of white raining down its side in some tribal language I'd never know or understand.

The animal bucked its horns at the gate a few times but must have caught the clown's colorful clothing and movement in its periphery because now it turned its head, then its entire body, kicking up dust with one of its back legs. It tucked its head between its dusty shoulders like a linebacker about to block a play.

As I watched all of this slowly unfolding, the announcer yelled through the overhead speakers: "And that, ladies and gentlemen, was Clyde Tuller from Mount Hermon. Give 'im a hand!"

The crowd erupted into applause for the young cowboy who had made it safely over the rail, but then all of their attention seemed to shift back to the arena where the bull was nudging at the dirt with his snout and kicking up clods of dust with his cracked black hoof.

The clown looked from side to side as he seemed to become aware of the bull's impending charge, but the noise from the crowd must have given him a surge of adrenaline because for a moment the clown just stood there smiling. Challenging the animal. The bull blew hot air onto the ground from its giant nostrils, like two black discs that if you looked into them you could probably see the bull's tiny brain inside its head, the primitive and angered thoughts that ran across the highways of synapses the only thing there to light it up. This was rage.

Then the bull charged.

The crowd stood as if connected to a single thread, which was suddenly pulled taut by some invisible ventriloquist who lifted them all upward to their collective feet.

I just stood there, completely transfixed as the bull drew nearer and nearer to the clown. But still the man never moved. He just waited, it seemed, to be gored, to become a human spectacle for the crowd—like the gladiators in Roman times: those terrible godless heathens. Pagans, my dad called them. And I wondered now what my dad was thinking about all of this; I was surprised that he was even watching it, but figured it would later just become another part of his lecture about the End Times, yet another bullet-point in his dissertation on how we were all doomed to Hell.

Just as the bull approached the sad, grizzled clown in the center of the arena—the noise from the crowd surging and pulsing under the sound of the announcer like waves coming ashore, the flood-lights hanging from the rafters overhead, casting an almost blue halo of light onto both man and bull below, limning it all under a scrim of gauze—the world seemed to pause for a moment. I stood there as though I were inside of a fat cumulus cloud, blinded by its glare.

Then that feeling of stillness snapped. It was like flicking a light switch or popping a rubber band—just like when I had thrown that dart earlier and knew it was going to hit the balloon. But this time I was suddenly back in the arena, watching the clown, who was now running across the dirt, the bull getting closer and closer. The crowd was still on its feet, yelling and laughing and throwing their food into the pen like wild animals in a cage at a zoo.

When the clown somehow finally made it to the metal gate and was then pulled up by each of his flanneled arms by two waiting cowboys—flinging his legs over just in time as the bull rammed its horns into the bars, whose force lifted the entire structure almost two feet from the ground—the mood of the crowd quelled, then seemed to turn to anger. They booed and threw more paper cups and beer cans and popcorn, a confetti of garbage and waste.

I looked over at my dad and could see him shaking his head, the lone audience member who was not participating in their protest. He reminded me of one of those assassins you see in pictures taken just before the fatal shot is fired—the smiling crowd waving and excited at the arrival of some important person, but that one face somber, eyes cold and calculating before doing what he had gone there to do. And no one ever noticed him until it was too late.

My dad started coming down the bleachers after he saw me standing at the entrance to the arena. When he reached me, he asked if I was ready.

"Yes, sir," I told him.

I saw him look down at my waistline where I had clipped my knife to my jeans. He shook his head again, then told me to come on.

"Okay," I said. "Thanks for bringing me here."

My dad didn't say anything.

I don't know if he even heard me over the din from the arena, but I followed him out of there, then through the midway, then beneath the gates of the fairgrounds, where we walked among the ebb and flow of revelers and then back to our truck in silence. He never asked to see my comic strip. And none of us brought it up again.

9

After that night my parents decided it was time for me to get baptized. I overhead them discussing it at the kitchen table the morning after the fair, one of the rare moments when they weren't fighting or otherwise sitting silently in separate rooms.

My dad said he was disturbed by all that had happened: the rodeo, how he had gone into my room after we got home and had taken my knife while I was sleeping. When I heard him say this, I looked over at my rickety night table where I had placed the knife before going to sleep and saw that it was indeed gone. My mother didn't ask him how I had even gotten a knife in the first place, and my dad didn't tell her. He also didn't say what he had done with it.

He was focused instead on talking to my mother about who would baptize me.

"You know I can just do it," my dad said.

"So could I," my mother said, "but that doesn't mean either one of us should. Don't you think it would be better to have a leader of the church baptize him?"

"Better in what way?"

"I don't know. Just more official."

"Rebekah, it doesn't say anywhere in the Bible that you have to be a leader of a church to baptize someone."

"Well," my mother said, "I guess it wouldn't be so bad if we did it." Then I heard her slide her chair back and start picking up dishes from off the kitchen table, placing them on the counter and turning on the sink, the sound of the basin slowly filling with what I imagined to be warm, soapy water. Even though I was in my room, I could still hear what was going on. I don't know if my parents knew this, but the walls in that old house were pretty thin.

My mother continued, "But I think we should still have him baptized at a church at some point. If we can ever find one that doesn't offend you." She said this with a hint of sarcasm, but my dad seemed to ignore it.

He just said, "Okay," and then I heard his chair scrape against the linoleum floor. A few seconds later, I heard his feet trudging down the hallway toward my room. Then he opened my door. I was lying in bed, pretending to read one of my home-school textbooks, when he came in and said, "Eli, why don't you come out to the kitchen? Your mother and I want to talk to you about something."

"Okay." I wanted to ask him about my knife, but figured it was best to let it go. I had already pushed my luck the past few days with that dumb comic strip. So I just got up and followed him down the hall.

In the kitchen, my mother was still washing dishes, a veil of steam coming up from the sink and surrounding her as she stood with her back turned to us. My dad and I sat down at the table.

"Rebekah, why don't you come sit with us? Talk to Eli about what we just discussed."

My mother turned off the water and wiped her hands on a stained dishtowel that was hanging from the handle on the stove. Then she came to the table and pulled out her chair, sat down.

"So," my dad began. "Your mother and I were thinking it's time you were baptized. You're almost thirteen. Definitely old enough now, and it's important to us; and it will be to you as well some day. Do you think you're ready for that responsibility?"

"I guess so," I said, not really understanding what being baptized had to do with responsibility, but I certainly wasn't going to tell my parents that.

"Good," my dad said. "I'm going to go outside and get ready. I'll call for you in a little while, okay?"

"Wow, John, you don't waste any time, do you?" my mother said.

"Well, what's there to think about, Rebekah? We both already agreed on this, and the boy said he's ready."

"I know, but it seems like there should be some kind of cere-mony. Something to make it feel more—I don't know—special, or something."

My dad didn't say anything. Already I could feel the tension in the kitchen building up, like someone stretching a piece of fabric until it was about to tear. This is how it always was with my parents: a seemingly minor thing could quickly escalate into a violent argu-ment with little provocation or warning. I didn't want to see that happen, so I took it upon myself to stand up. I just said, "It's okay. I'm ready."

Both my parents looked over at me, as if they had momentarily forgotten I was there.

"See?" my dad said. "He's ready."

And like that the three of us were walking outside into the front yard. It was midmorning and the sky was bright blue where the sun washed over it, outlining the trees, which themselves looked like a bunch of black paintbrushes pointing up and coloring the atmosphere. The air was thick with humidity and still. Hardly a breeze stirred.

The field stretched out before us, looking more like a giant green saucer pocked with a couple of small brown ponds and some trees. I wondered where we were going, exactly, and what this baptism would be like. I knew there was a river beyond the woods, but I couldn't imagine we would be walking that far. My parents were mostly quiet, and save for the noise of the cows in the distance, all was silent.

I kept thinking about this short story by Langston Hughes that my parents had made me read once. It was called "Salvation" and it was about this little boy not getting saved because he couldn't see Jesus. In the end, he just lay in his bed alone and unsaved, crying himself to sleep.

I said to my parents that I felt sorry for the little boy because he didn't see Jesus and how his friends were all mean to him about it. But my dad told me how the little boy was actually special because he was like the one sheep that Jesus talked about in the book of Matthew, the one who strayed from the flock, but was ultimately brought back into the fold—they told me that those other nine-ty-nine sheep were all alike, but this little boy's salvation would be more important when it finally did happen because he really thought about what it all meant. It wasn't a sad ending, they told me. It was a happy one because the little boy was analyzing his circumstances. And that's what they wanted me to learn, they said: to be a critical thinker.

As we walked toward the pasture, I tried to imagine what was going to happen to me when I was baptized. But I wasn't able to come to any real conclusions about it. So I just kept following my parents as they both walked over to the fence line that bordered our small yard and then went through the little opening that led into the field.

We tried to be careful as we moved over the rusty cattle guard and toward the wide-open pasture, where a metal trough that belonged to Mr. Tally—which the cows drank out of during the day—sat on the ground like a large boulder in the middle of the knee-high grass.

"So you want to baptize our son in a cattle trough?" my mother said. "Why not just assign his soul to Purgatory instead?"

"God help us, Rebekah, don't you ever quit?"

My mother didn't say anything, but she smiled. She seemed delighted by her own wit.

The sun was getting brighter as we stood there. My parents were both quiet now, visibly annoyed with one another, and I felt nervous standing there in the dirt with no shoes or socks on my feet, several lethargic cows looming in the distance, not too far from where we were standing next to their trough. It was as if they were watching this strange spectacle that was about to take place, waiting to see what would happen.

"Come on, son," my dad said, motioning me toward the trough. I walked over to it, looked down at the giant metal tub, the water still and cool and pocked with bits of grass and hay, skeins of dust on its surface like continents sketched out on a map. I could see the reflection of the sun shining against the corrugated metal sides of the tub and the smooth dark water as though it were looking back at me.

I stood beside my dad.

"Now why don't you just go ahead and climb in there," he said.

"In there?"

"Well, what did you think we came all the way out here for?" he said. "To stare at the cows?"

"No, but I didn't know I'd have to do that."

Then my mother spoke: "John, why don't we just do this at a church? Like normal people? Eli," she said, looking over at me now, "you don't have to do this."

"Rebekah, please don't contradict me in front of our son. We've come out here with a purpose this morning, and I mean to fulfill it."

I didn't want my parents to start fighting again, so I just agreed to get in the cattle trough to be baptized. The water was cold on my bare feet and legs, then seemed to wrap itself around me as I sank down into it. The trough wasn't very big, so I had to sit with my knees bent, and even still the water barely came up to my chest. I could feel my heart beating. I waited.

My parents came over to me and I saw their faces outlined against the sky behind them. I looked up, shivering, even though it was hot outside, and despite this supposedly being a safe and comforting event.

Then I looked down at the water, which was undulating slightly with each anxious breath I took. Now I could see my own reflection on the water's surface, pulsing up and down like a tide coming in over a river's soft shoals. Several of the cows had started to amble in toward us. I could feel their presence behind my parents, still and looming and curious.

My dad looked up at the sky, silent at first as if in prayer, then speaking finally as if directly to the heavens. "This, Yahuwah, is my son, Eli Woodbine, and he comes today to be baptized unto You, and in Your name."

My mother moved in closer. "Amen," she said. She was looking down at me and I could see now that her cheeks were suddenly shining with a stream of fresh, real tears. I wondered if she was crying because she was sad, or if she was actually happy that this was happening to me.

"Now, Eli," my dad said. "Please repeat these words after me."

I nodded.

"I believe."

"I believe."

"That Jesus is the Son of Yahuwah."

"That Jesus is the Son of Yahuwah."

"My Lord."

"My Lord."

"And my savior."

"And my savior."

I had my arms outstretched and was gripping the cool sides of the trough as I spoke. I no longer felt cold, but could still hear my heart beating in my head, punctuating in my skull the echo of this solemn call and response.

When my dad placed his hand on my forehead, though, I didn't know it was in preparation to push me under the water. He gave me no warning of this, and his movement was so stern, so quick, that I had no time to prepare myself for what was about to happen. He pushed me down and I went under with my mouth open—just as I was taking in a breath of the still, humid air outside the trough. And suddenly that warm air was replaced with a mouthful of stinging water as it went down my throat and seemed to enter my lungs. I flailed my arms and legs, trying to rise above the surface.

For a moment everything went black.

And then I felt my dad's hand move away from my forehead, leaving me free to come up on my own, where I choked and coughed out water and phlegm into the trough and then over the side into the grass. It splattered into the dust and onto my parents' feet. They stepped away to avoid the mess, then quickly returned to help me out of the trough.

"Eli, are you all right?" my mother said, shouting loud enough so that several of the cows who had been looming over us twitched, started to shoulder away and to someplace more quiet.

I was still coughing and choking, so I didn't answer her, but I tried to shake my head yes and stand up so that I could get out of the tub. I was ready to go back home.

My dad was helping me up, smacking his cold wet palm against my back, where it made a loud clapping sound against my soaked shirt. The fabric was stuck to my skin like a plastic bag that had been blown against a telephone pole, and my dad's hand hitting it sounded like someone slapping a wet towel at a tree.

I climbed out of the trough and onto the dirt on my uncertain knees, the dust powdering my bare feet and ankles, then becoming caked there as it mixed with the water, which dripped off of me as though I had just come inside from a terrible rainstorm.

"I'm sorry, son," my dad said. "I thought you were ready." I wasn't sure if he meant that literally or figuratively. Regardless, he would have been wrong in either sense. Like the little boy in that Langston Hughes story, I hadn't been saved. Like him, I guess I hadn't been ready after all.

Then my mother turned on him. "Jesus Christ, John, what were trying to do? Drown him? I swear you cannot do a fucking thing right."

"Rebekah, please don't. Let's just go back to the house. We can talk about this inside."

"That's easy for you to say. Look at him!" My mother pointed at me. I imagined from her perspective that I must have looked like a waif standing there dripping water, my wet clothes stuck to my body, no shoes or socks, my hair a tangled, drenched nest.

The cows had been thoroughly startled now and had all moved away from us so that it was just my parents and me standing next to the trough. I looked up and then toward Mr. Tally's house off in the distance. I could see a silhouette of someone coming out onto the porch, appearing to look out at us where we stood in the field.

Then the figure's arm seemed to come up toward its head, shading its eyes from the sun, probably to see what was happening over here: these three silhouettes standing next to an animal trough among a passel of skulking cows.

I figured it would be just a matter of minutes before we heard Mr. Tally's four-wheeler start up. Then he would come over to us to see what was happening. It wouldn't be the first time I was embarrassed like that by my parents, but I really didn't want Mr. Tally to see me like this, all drenched and shaking and cold. And unsaved.

My parents, seeing me staring off in that direction, both turned to see what I was looking at.

"Come on, Rebekah, let's just get back to the house," my dad said, grabbing my mother's arm. "Before Tally comes over here and starts asking me why I'm not working."

Then he turned to me. "Are you sure you're okay, Eli?"

"Yes," I said. "I'm fine."

"Good. Well, come on then."

As we started to walk back across the field and to our house, my parents continued to fight.

"You didn't even bring a towel for him to dry off with," my mother said. "If he gets sick, you're going to stay inside with him all day. Not me. I had things I wanted to get done today too. This was never part of my plan, I can tell you that."

My dad didn't say anything, and we all just kept walking through the field, the high grass brushing against our shins and making a whispering sound against my dad's tan Dickies work pants. He was clenching his jaw, trying, it seemed, to keep from letting his anger erupt over and onto my mother, who still kept prodding at him—she was like a leafless branch worrying against the side of a house in a storm.

"How can anyone function in this environment, John? Huh? Can you tell me that? With everything I do, all I ask for is a little bit of peace. And you can't even grant me one morning without having to clean up one of your stupid messes."

My dad kept walking, but he was moving faster now across the field. Our house loomed in the distance.

"And look at our son," she kept on. "He's soaking wet. Jesus, sometimes I truly wonder what I must have done in some past life to deserve being married to you."

I walked beside my parents, kept my arms crossed over my chest, silent, trying to hold the warmth against my body as we continued to make our way through the field. As usual, I felt guilty—felt as though it were my fault that all of this was happening. As though my parents would have been so much happier if it weren't for me. Had I not sent off that comic, we would have never gone to the fair, my dad never would have felt compelled to baptize me, and we would be existing just as we always had before.

I looked back toward Mr. Tally's house, and since I couldn't hear his four-wheeler like I had expected, I figured he had gone back inside.

Maybe he wouldn't come over and confront my parents about seeing them dunk me underwater in the cow trough. Maybe he wouldn't ask my dad why he wasn't out working instead of trying to baptize his son in the field, his son who should have been in school, socializing with other kids his age. I had heard conversations like this before between my dad and Mr. Tally, and I knew that the last thing any of us needed that morning was another fight. I was grateful he hadn't come out.

When we got to the porch, my dad told me to wait outside until he went in and got a towel. My mother went in ahead of him, letting the screen door smack shut dramatically against the doorframe.

I stood there on the porch, still shivering despite the heat and the unmoving humid air around us. Then I sat down with my feet dangling from the rickety porch boards, and I thought about what had just happened. I wondered if my dad would be disappointed in me or in himself for our failed baptism.

After all that I had heard about baptisms from the bits of Scripture my dad read to me about John and about Christ, the person baptizing you was supposed to say something at the end like, "I now baptize you, for the forgiveness of your sins, in the name of the Father, the Son, and the Holy Spirit. Amen." My dad hadn't said that. And I had almost drowned. I wondered what that incompletion might end up meaning for my soul. Would it go to Purgatory, or worse, to Hell? Was I really like the little boy in the Langston Hughes story now because I hadn't seen Jesus? Was I supposed to have seen him? I couldn't remember either if it said anything in the Bible about an incomplete baptism—what that meant for someone who was at the receiving end of one, or if there had ever been a case like this before, one in which the person had almost drowned before the ceremony was done.

When my dad came back out to the porch, he handed me a large bath towel and told me to dry off. I stood and wrapped the towel around myself, covering my head and part of my face with it so that I must have looked like one of Christ's own disciples. Only I wasn't dressed to ward off the desert sun and heat as I walked the earth to spread the gospel, keeping my face in shadow; I was soaked and freezing from being dunked by my dad into a cow trough, and now I was standing on the slanted porch of a house we didn't even own, couldn't afford to pay rent on half the time, and waiting for my dad to say something to me or otherwise go back inside. Something. Anything to indicate this humiliation would finally be over.

But my dad didn't do either.

Instead, he just stood there, watching me as I dried first my hair and then the rest of my body, pressing the towel into my wet clothes to soak up some of the water so that I could go inside and not drip all over the house on my way to the bathroom.

After a minute, my dad walked across the porch and sat in his rocking chair, lighting one of his pipes, the sweet smell of burning tobacco wafting up and hovering just under the drooping porch fan, its rusty blades bent downward by the humidity like over-watered flower petals. I heard the wooden arcs at the base of the rocking chair as they creaked over the porch boards, my dad slowly moving back and forth, looking out at the field and beyond that, Mr. Tally's barn and farmhouse, which stood silent under the haze rising up from the sloping field.

Even from here, you could almost make out the silhouettes of Mr. Tally and his family behind the uncurtained windows as they moved around inside their house, most likely preparing for lunch.

My parents and I had been to lunch over there before—just once, though—and I remember it had been everything I had always imagined it would be: red and white checkered cloths on the table, fresh cold milk served in Mason jars, homemade biscuits puffing out of a little wicker basket like large mushrooms, fried chicken, and ears of buttered corn straight from their own garden out back.

I remember Mr. Tally, his wife, and his twin five-year-old daughters sitting at the table and how when Mr. Tally began to say grace, my dad had stood up and objected to something Mr. Tally had said in his invocation of the Lord and his thanks for his family and the meal that we all were about to share. He said it was sacrilege, blasphemy, how he wasn't worthy of uttering the name of the Lord, something so great and majestic that it was beyond our human language to comprehend or express. It was vanity that compelled us to even try, he said. I remember him slamming his hands on the table and how the milk shook in the Mason jars and almost spilled from the sweating carafe in the center of the table.

Mrs. Tally had kept her head down during this exchange, while her twin daughters looked utterly frightened in their Sunday dresses. They were so young they probably didn't understand what was even happening. But I knew they would probably never forget it, my dad standing in their dining room—yelling, pounding his fists on the table like the angry preacher he probably wished he was. I was just happy those little girls weren't closer to me in age; at least they were too young for me to be thoroughly embarrassed in front of them.

My mother had put her hand on my dad's arm. "John," she said softly, trying to hide what was likely her own embarrassment. "Please sit down and let's just enjoy this meal. Please. This is not our home. You work for this man. Please."

My dad looked at her, then over at me, then finally at Mr. Tally, who was watching him cautiously. Mr. Tally hadn't stood, but remained at the head of his table.

"I'm sorry," my mother said. "My husband doesn't mean any disrespect. He's just very passionate is all."

Mr. Tally immediately tried to brighten up the mood. "Well, I can appreciate a little emotion," he said. "Hopefully, that passion will find its way into the work you do here too. Lord knows we can use it."

At that time, we had been living there for only a couple of days and I think Mr. Tally was trying to remain optimistic about his decision to hire my dad to work his land. We had already moved in to the little house at the edge of his field, and it would have been a huge inconvenience for him to kick us out now.

It also wasn't lost on me that Mr. Tally had used the word "Lord," as if to reassert his position as the owner of this land and as my dad's boss. It was as though he were trying to say that he would utter God's name in his own house whenever he pleased. And in that moment, I felt a certain warmth toward him that would only grow during our time living on his farm.

Mr. Tally's wife smiled, picked up the little wicker basket overflowing with warm biscuits, and then she passed the basket to my mother, who took it without looking up from the table.

After that we all started passing around plates of steaming food, and I ate better that afternoon than I ever had before—or since. I had always admired Mr. Tally for that, for his ability to extinguish the fire my dad so clearly had hoped to start that day, and on many other occasions like it. But I remember this too: Mr. Tally had never invited our family back to his house for another meal again.

Yet ever since that afternoon, around this time, I would imagine what seemed to be such an idyllic scene taking place, how my family was perpetually outside of that scene, like watching a movie about a perfect family while, on the other side of the screen, your own was falling apart.

10

I was mostly dry when I started to walk back across the porch and into the house. But first I looked over at my dad, who was still rocking in his chair and puffing leisurely on his pipe, the wooden bowl lighting up orange and then fading to black, then gray as the tobacco burned and popped and hissed. He didn't say anything, just nodded his head at me like one of the old men who sat outside the convenience store in town, as if I were someone he saw every day, but had no idea who I really was.

I nodded back at him and went inside, where I walked to the bathroom and stripped off my wet clothes, dropped them onto the floor, and took a hot shower to warm myself up. When I was finished, I got dressed and went outside to hang my wet clothes on the line to dry.

When my dad saw me standing in front of the clothesline hanging my damp shirt and pants, he asked if I would help him catch one of the fat white hens that were wobbling around in our yard so that we could have something decent for lunch. Mr. Tally had told my dad that we could have the chickens, which had been left behind by the previous tenants, as long as we fed and watered them, collected their eggs every morning.

This had been my responsibility, and I never minded doing it. I actually enjoyed having a sense of purpose during those otherwise amorphous days of being home-schooled, days during which time seemed to almost cease to exist. Those long hours sitting in my room with no sense of a schedule or a format to the day, staring at books or out of my window, daydreaming, which always seemed to make me think of that weird painting with the melting clocks:

the hours and minutes and seconds dripping like a leaky faucet, how one day bled into the next with no delineation or demarcation whatsoever.

But now—almost as if he had read my mind earlier when I had been thinking about that first-and-only disastrous lunch at Mr. Tally's house and how part of me still longed to recreate it, or something like it at least—my dad was saying that he wanted me to help him kill one of our chickens so that my mother could fry it for a special supper they wanted to have later that evening.

To celebrate my being baptized, he had said. I guessed that meant it was official then, even though he hadn't finished all the words during the ceremony. Maybe it was like what he had said about the name of God, that some things were simply unutterable. I knew this should've made me feel better, but it didn't. When it came to religion, instead of being a source of comfort, it was just more uncertainty in my life, a sense of being either right or wrong, but never really knowing anything at all so that you were always full of doubt and afraid.

Before I had come outside to hang up my wet clothes, my dad had been just outside my bedroom window chopping firewood. Despite the heat, my window was open, and I could hear him as I sat in my bed.

I could hear the metal hatchet as it split the logs, punctuated by the occasional grunting noises my dad made as he picked up the wood and placed it on the stump to split it. The wood he was chopping was from an old oak tree that a man named Mr. Brumfield had cut down a couple of weeks earlier. Mr. Brumfield was an old man who owned the property next to where we lived, and Mr. Tally's land was divided from his by a stretch of rusty barbed-wire fence.

One morning while he was out in the fields doing work for Mr. Tally, my dad saw the felled tree next to the fence line and asked Mr. Brumfield if he could have it. Mr. Brumfield told my dad that as long as we got it off his property, he didn't care what we did with that old tree.

So I rode with my dad across the field in his pickup truck one afternoon and I watched as he took a chainsaw and cut the giant tree up into manageable pieces. Then I helped him load them into the back of his truck and we drove the tree, piece by piece back to our house, where we unloaded all of it into our yard. It took about eight or nine trips to get it all moved.

After that, my dad would spend each afternoon chopping up the wood and stacking cord upon cord of it next to our house, covering the piles with sheets of muddy Visqueen. It had become almost like an obsession for him, that work. Anything to keep from being still. He said that he had planned to sell most of it that winter and that we'd use the rest of it to heat our house if it got cold enough outside. If it didn't, he'd find something else to do with it all, he'd said.

Mr. Tally offered to buy some of the firewood from us, and one day I overheard my dad making an agreement with him in which he would just exchange a few cords of wood for the cost of what we still owed on the rent that month. This was a very generous deal, one even I could recognize. Mr. Tally also never said anything about my dad neglecting some of his farm duties to hang out in the yard and chop wood all day.

So by the afternoon of my failed baptism, he probably had about a half-dozen cords of firewood, all covered with tarps or pieces of plywood or rusty sheets of roofing tin—whatever he could find to keep the rain off of it. And he was almost finished with this job, which had taken him a couple of days to complete, when he stopped what he was doing to ask me to help him catch and kill one of our chickens.

But now the problem was this: I had never killed an animal before. My dad had never taken me hunting or fishing, and even though we had about a dozen chickens, the idea of eating one of them had never been brought up until that day. I had never heard my parents discuss this as something we would ever do. So, just as I had felt before my baptism earlier that morning, I was once again simultaneously excited and nervous about the prospect of what was going to happen.

I helped my dad cover up the last cord of firewood with a piece of Visqueen and watched as he picked up the rusty hatchet he had been using to split the oak branches. Then he told me to follow him and we walked back to the chicken coop where some of the hens were walking around just outside on the dirty, grassless patch of land surrounding it, pecking at the spray of corn seeds that were spangled in the mud. A couple of them were perched inside the coop and nesting in a pile of yellow hay, warming the very eggs that I would probably have to come back out later to collect.

The one rooster we had was standing just outside the coop's opening, surveying the hens. The good thing was that most of the chickens were pretty big so it wasn't difficult to choose one. My dad simply walked over to the closest hen—a golden brown one whose waxy feathers seemed to shine in the sunlight—and picked it up. The hen clucked and flapped its wings but my dad held tight with both hands, the hatchet still in his right hand, its wooden handle pressed against the hen's side as he walked it over to the same stump where he had been chopping firewood just a few minutes earlier.

"Eli, come over here," he said. I was still standing near the coop, watching the other hens peck at the pellets of corn. I wondered if they had any idea what was going on, if they could anticipate with their tiny brains what was about to happen. And if they could, would they even care? None of them seemed to notice anything amiss.

"Okay," I said. I walked over to where my dad was standing next to the stump, holding the hen in place. Then he handed me the hatchet.

He said, "I'm going to hold her head down, and I want you to chop it off when I tell you to, okay?"

"Can I hold her and you do it?" I said.

"No," he said. "You need to start learning how to do these kinds of things yourself, Eli. One day I might not be here, and then what are you going to do?"

Then he pushed the hen down on her side and held her head against the stump. You could see the gashes from where the hatchet had gone into the stump's surface countless times before. They surrounded the hen like knife cuts on someone's skin. The chicken clucked and her scaled feet moved as though she were running. Her feathers twitched under my dad's thick, hairy fingers.

"Come on," he said. "Do it. Before she gets away."

I raised the hatchet up, imagining for a brief moment accidentally hitting my dad's wrist with the sharpened, rusty bit, but then, before I could think about anything else, I squinted my eyes and brought the blade down onto the hen's neck. Quick and hard. The edge of the hatchet went easily through her throat and the flesh encasing it, then into the wooden stump beneath her, a quick spray of dark blood spilling forth, pooling around in the little space that now separated her head from her body. The legs and feathers continued to twitch but my dad let the hen go.

I watched in shock as the hen stood, then flapped her wings until she was off the stump. Now she was on the ground, running blindly in what looked to be drunken circles among the clumps of brown grass, dirt, and chips of wood left over from the chopped-up oak tree.

My dad laughed. "Don't worry," he said. "You didn't do anything wrong. This happens almost every time. The nerves in her body are still firing, that's all. She can't feel anything. Believe me."

By now, one of Mr. Tally's dogs had skulked over into the yard, probably at the smell of blood, and it was sniffing curiously at the headless bird that was still running around in wild, erratic circles, flapping its wings uselessly against the dust and the grass. The other hens and the rooster still went about clucking and milling around the corn seed next to their coop. To them, it seemed as though nothing at all out of the ordinary had happened.

Finally, after a couple of minutes, the hen fell over and twitched several more times before becoming completely still. More blood leaked from the hole where its head had once been. The blood pooled black, with a skein of gray dust on its surface like pepper sprinkled over a bowl of thick dark soup.

My dad went over and picked up the hen's body, then brought it back over to where I was standing, my mouth hanging open as though my jaw had become unhinged from the rest of my skull. I watched him push the head off of the stump with his hand, then place the hen's body on the bloody surface that was normally meant for chopping wood. The dog that had been until now cautiously surveying the scene, finally picked up the disembodied head and ran off under our house with it.

"Hand me that hatchet, will you?" my dad said. I was still trying to process all that I had just witnessed and hadn't realized I was still holding the killing tool in my quivering hand. I turned to give it to him, then watched as he wiped some blood and a few tiny feathers from the blade and onto his flannel shirt. He put the hatchet in his belt.

"Okay," he said. "Now I want you to come pluck off these feathers. You don't have to worry about getting all of them. Just the big ones for now."

The air around us had a bitter, coppery smell and I tried to hold my breath so I wouldn't gag. I thought about how that knife I had won at the fair the night before would be useful right about then, but I was afraid to bring it up. For all I knew, he had already thrown it away, a bad memory for him now like the fair itself, becoming more and more distant in his mind with each passing minute. I just walked over to the hen and started tearing out her feathers like I had been told.

"Good," my dad was saying as I pulled and pulled. The sound was like tearing the sleeves off of a flannel shirt. You could hear the ripping as the feathers came away from the pink, mottled flesh. My dad watched me do this for a second, then said he was going to go get a bucket from the shed, that he'd be back in a minute. Told me to just keep plucking.

As I plucked the chicken, tossing the feathers onto the ground, I was no longer hungry. I couldn't imagine eating this animal I had just killed and then watched run around, headless, in our yard. I tried to think of how I could tell this to my dad without him being mad or disappointed in me.

I was still pulling out the dead chicken's feathers and thinking about not eating her when I heard my dad coming out of the shed, a metal bucket banging against his thigh as he went over to the spigot and filled the bucket up with water. He came back to where I was and put the bucket down, then walked to one of the burn piles that were pocked throughout the yard and lit it with a match and some newspaper. I watched him as he covered the small flame with a rusty metal grate that he used for cooking. He set the bucket on top of that.

By the time I started to hear the water boiling, I was finished plucking the hen and my dad told me to bring the body over and to drop it into the bucket.

"To remove the rest of the feathers," he said, seeming to notice my confusion at what he was asking me to do.

"Those little white ones that are so hard to pluck," he continued, "those are called down feathers. And this boiling water will make them slide right off, like butter on a hot sidewalk." He smiled at what he probably thought was as an interesting image he had just conjured. But I was still too shocked to appreciate anything that was happening just then. So I just stood there, holding the dead chicken in my bloodied hands.

"Look, don't worry about it, Eli, okay?" my dad said, taking the hen from me and dropping it into the bucket of boiling water. "After this, all we'll have to do is cut her up so Mom can cook it later."

I knew he was trying to teach me something by showing me all of this, but I didn't know why everything we did had to be so primitive. Both of my parents had talked a lot about the End Times being upon us and how we had to be ready for them, so I imagined this was part of their logic, but sometimes I really wished we could've just gone to the Jr. Food Mart down the road and just buy a box of fried chicken like normal people did.

I stood over the bucket and watched the water envelop the chicken's body, the bubbles disappearing for a moment as the hen sank to the bottom. Then my dad picked up the bucket by its handle and walked back over to the stump. I watched him as he scraped the remaining specks of blood and feathers off of the stump's surface with his boot, then dumped the steaming water onto the place where we had just killed and plucked the hen. The boiling water laved the stump clean as the hen's limp body oozed out of the bucket, where it finally rested in a heap of smoking pink flesh.

My dad took the hatchet from where he had placed it in his belt and wiped the blade against his jeans. Then he used it to chop off the hen's legs and wings, her neck. Finally, he reached in and pulled out a handful of dark entrails, tossing them onto the ground.

By now some of the other chickens had started to come over and were pecking curiously at the bloody mess in the dirt. The rooster actually picked up a stringy piece of gray intestine and ran off with it dangling from his beak. The other hens just pecked and pecked at the carnage, as if they might divine something about their own existences from all this blood and feathers.

"Disgusting creatures," my dad said, shaking his head and then lifting his hatchet again so he could start quartering the breast and thighs.

I watched him and tried not to look at the other chickens, who themselves might one day meet this same awful fate. And what made it so much worse was how oblivious they all seemed, how almost blissful they were as they pecked away at the mound of damp guts.

"There," my dad finally said. He put the hatchet back into his belt. "This should be good." He picked up the wings and other edible parts and put them all back in the bucket. "Now let's bring this inside so your mother can cook it. I'm starving."

11

We walked across the yard and to the porch. When we got inside, I could see that my mother had already set up the kitchen for supper. On the counter were several plates, each one covered with a paper towel that was blanketed with a skein of flour. Behind her on the stovetop was a cast-iron skillet, already sizzling with a layer of cooking oil. The kitchen window was open and the little curtain was whispering in the light breeze that was coming in from the yard.

"Here you go," my dad said, placing the dirty bucket on the counter. My mother was at the sink, washing her hands and staring out the open window. Then she turned around. Her eyes were wide, as though someone had just poured cold water over her head.

"John, what is that?" she said.

"It's the chicken."

"In a metal bucket?"

"Well, what did you want us to do with it? Carry in a bunch of loose parts? The dog's already going berserk out there as it is."

"Oh my God." My mother started to walk toward the counter, leaving the sink running behind her; then she tilted the bucket and looked inside of it. I knew it wasn't particularly clean, as my dad put it to various uses around the farm, but he never seemed to care about those sorts of things. It drove my mother crazy.

"John," she said, "is there no end to how you'll try and try and try to make my life miserable? Is there just no end?"

"Oh, come on, Rebekah, not right now, okay? I just got inside. Can we just not do this again?"

My mother picked up the bucket, started to shake the chicken parts out and onto the counter. She picked up one of the drumsticks and rolled it around theatrically in the flour. Then she tossed it into the pan of grease. It bubbled furiously.

"Is this what you want? The obedient little wife to do her chores?" She was picking up the chicken parts and dropping them in the mounds of flour, then grabbing handfuls of the powder and dousing the meat with it. Flour was getting everywhere: on her clothes, the counter, the floor. She reached up to push back a strand of hair and inadvertently traced a line of flour across her cheek.

I just stood there, my hands by my sides, and watched as my mother tossed piece after piece of chicken into the popping skillet. Brown grease splattered onto the stove and steam rose into the air and went out the window. All I wanted then was to go back to my room and be alone, away from my parents.

"Look, Rebekah," my dad said, trying to calm her. "Why don't you just go sit in the den, okay? I'll take care of this. You really need to settle down. I'm really starting to worry about your behavior."

My mother stood there, staring, streaks of white flour across her sweat-glistened face.

Then my dad walked into the heart of the kitchen next to the stove and nudged my mother gently out of the way. He slowly and deliberately took the last couple of pieces of chicken out of the bucket and started coating them with flour. I watched him as he turned and lowered the heat on the stove, using a pair of metal tongs to flip the chicken that was already in the skillet. The grease started to settle down, but still it hissed and popped as the meat fried.

I watched, waiting to see what would happen.

"Eli," my dad said, speaking calmly. I could tell by how taut his lips were against his teeth as he spoke that he was trying to maintain the appearance of control and order, of being calm. "Can you take this bucket outside and rinse it out for me?"

"Sure," I said. I was just happy to have an excuse to get out of the house. He could've asked me to do anything just then and I would have agreed.

My mother was still standing in front of the counter, her shirt and hands covered with flour, her eyes wide and darting around the room. I tried not to look at her. Instead, I went and picked up the bucket and started to go outside with it. I opened the screen door and walked out onto the porch. I could hear Mr. Tally's dog under the floorboards, still gnawing and slobbering on the chicken parts he had pilfered earlier.

I walked across the yard and turned on the spigot next to where my dad and I had been chopping wood, then filled the bucket halfway with water before swishing it around some to get the dirt and blood off the sides. I took my hand and rubbed the inside walls of the bucket, then dumped out the dirty water onto the ground, where it was soaked up almost completely by the dry earth.

After that, I turned off the spigot and placed the bucket face up on top of the stump—the one on which we had killed the chicken earlier—so that it could dry out in the sun. As I turned to walk back, I heard my mother yelling and then I saw the screen door come open so violently that it hit the outside wall of the house, and its rusty hinges squealed. Then I watched as the skillet full of hot grease and pieces of half-fried chicken came flying across the porch and landed in the grass.

I stood there, watching as Mr. Tally's dog came out from under the porch and nuzzled at the new pieces of meat before him, partially fried and steaming in the dirt. He sniffed at them and pushed the partially-fried chicken around with his paws.

Now I could hear my parents inside of the house throwing things around, yelling at each other about "shared responsibility," the role of a good wife and a supportive husband. Then I saw my dad walk slowly and dejectedly out onto the porch, my mother still yelling at him from inside. He gentled the screen door shut, which seemed to hang somewhat loosely on its hinges now, and walked down the steps. I watched him as he nudged the dog away with his shoe, then picked up the chicken and started putting the pieces back into the empty skillet.

He seemed to ignore me as he went over to the spigot I had just used to wash out the bucket and then he started rinsing the grass and dirt off of the chicken, rubbing the pieces of meat with his hand to get them cleaned. I wanted to help him, but knew it was best to leave him alone.

I walked across the yard, climbed over the fence, and went into Mr. Tally's field until I could no longer hear my mother's yelling, or the noise of my dad working obsessively to drown it out.

I sat out there by myself until it was nearly dark. By then I was pretty sure my parents had calmed down. I just hoped they hadn't broken any windows or doors. I didn't know how we would have been able to afford paying Mr. Tally to have it all fixed, or if he'd even let us stay there at all anymore if my parents had broken anything. I figured they had probably just gone to their rooms though, closed the doors and casting the house in silence.

I walked back home. I could see that someone had turned on the porchlight, but inside it appeared dark, still, quiet. I could hear someone moving around in the shed out back, what sounded like a hacksaw blade going through a piece of wood. It was probably my dad, working so he wouldn't have to deal with the problems inside.

I ignored him, and instead went in the house and turned on the light in the den.

As I looked around, I could see the flour still coating almost every surface of the kitchen: the walls, the countertop, the stove. There was broken glass on the floor, a butcher's knife, pieces of half-cooked chicken. Flies buzzed around the one naked light bulb that was suspended from the ceiling at the end of a gray wire. I turned away, walked down the hall, and put my ear against my mother's closed bedroom door. I listened to her soft snoring for a minute, glad she seemed to be sleeping. Then I went back into the kitchen to clean up.

12

Things continued to get worse with my parents' fighting and so I started spending more time outside in the field with the cows and horses, more time in the woods where it was quiet and shaded and where I didn't have to hear their constant arguments, the dishes breaking, doors slamming. All I could do was go outside, get away, escape.

One night, not long after the incident with the chicken, I was in the field and about to go back to our house when I looked over at a herd of cows that were all standing completely still in the twilight. Occasionally, one of their tails would flicker. Their eyes were open, but they didn't look as active as they had during the day. I thought that the animals were sleeping. I had heard that they slept standing up, but I wasn't sure if that was true or not.

I had also heard about people knocking the cows over while they were in that state. It was called "cow tipping." I stood there and I thought about what it would be like to knock one of them over: just walk up to the sleeping animal and push it with all of my strength, then watch it fall down like one of those large bags of feed Mr. Tally would sometimes get my dad to toss out from the barn loft and into the back of his truck, the bag landing with a thud, a cloud of dust and dirt rising up from the truck bed as its axles settled against the weight.

I liked animals though and didn't want to hurt any of them, but

I was still curious, so that night I just walked over to the herd with the simple intention of trying to push one of the cows over. Just to see what would happen. As soon as some of them sensed me, though, they began to shift around in the dust. The moonlight was coming down through the trees and I could see the animals pretty well in the wash of light before me, their movements and shadows flickering on the field. Some of them still weren't moving, and I could tell they were sleeping, even though their eyes were open and glassy-looking.

I walked over to one of them and was about to push it when I heard Mr. Tally's four-wheeler coming across the pasture. I saw the white headlights skittering across the hills and swales, so I ducked down behind a tree and waited for him to pass.

Mr. Tally would occasionally drive the fields at night like that to check on his stock, or maybe it was just to get away from his house. I don't know. But I did know that I didn't want Mr. Tally to see me out there, so I stayed down and waited.

The four-wheeler kept coming. The headlights grew larger as it closed the distance between itself and me. Still I stood there, crouched and silent. Then I felt the headlights blanketing the clearing, completely covering my hiding place. The four-wheeler slowed and came to a stop and I heard Mr. Tally say, "Who's out there?"

At first I didn't answer.

"I done seen someone over here. Ain't no use in hiding. Come on out," he said.

I was still silent, trying to stay invisible beneath the wash of headlights and the dust being stirred up from the moving cows. I sat there. Waited.

Mr. Tally kept the headlights on as he climbed down from the four-wheeler. I could see his silhouette grabbing a shotgun from off the metal rack behind the seat. That's when I stood up and raised my hands.

"Mr. Tally," I said. "It's me. Please. Don't shoot."

"Who's that there?" he yelled over the noise of the four-wheeler, his disembodied voice coming across the air like someone revving a chainsaw in the woods. It was a noise you could hear from a great distance, though it felt as if the person with the saw was standing right in front of you. That's how Mr. Tally sounded then.

"It's me. Eli," I said.

"Eli?" He was closer to me now and had lowered his voice as he talked to me.

"Yes, sir," I said.

"What the hell are you doin' out here, bud?"

"Just walking around," I said. "I didn't mean to cause any trouble. I'm sorry."

"Well, this ain't such a good place to be walkin' around at night, son. You know that, right?"

"Yes, sir. I know. I'm sorry."

"Why don't you get on the four-wheeler and I'll ride you back to your place? I been meaning to talk to you anyway about somethin'."

"Okay," I said.

I could see the dust cloud settling in the white light of the four-wheeler, and I went over to it and climbed onto the seat. Mr. Tally walked over to the cows and looked at them for a second, ran his hand across one of their flanks. Then he walked back over to the four-wheeler, put the shotgun on the rack, and climbed on the seat in front of me. I could hear it creak under his weight, going up and down on its shocks as he rose from the seat a bit and reached into his shirt pocket to pull out a pack of cigarettes and a tiny box of matches.

I saw the match flame ignite, then the orange tip of the cigarette as he lit it. Everything was in silhouette, it seemed, except for the smoke, which still somehow looked gray in the night with the scrim of headlight behind it and the black trees and black shapes of the cows in the distance. It looked like one of those old black-and-white movies that came on late at night on PBS. Even though we didn't have a TV in our house, I sometimes could see into Mr. Tally's windows, and often he and his wife would watch movies that looked like that, their faces flickering in the soft glow from the television as they sat next to each other on the sofa.

After Mr. Tally had his cigarette lit, he returned the crumpled pack and his matches back inside of his shirt pocket, and then he sat back down on the seat in front of me and put the four-wheeler in reverse. As he backed it up and began to turn around, he looked over his shoulder at me and said, "I don't know how to say this but to just come right out with it," he said. "I think you're plenty old enough to hear it straight."

I didn't say anything, just listened. Then he put the four-wheeler into drive and started slowly over the field toward where our tiny house was situated at the edge of the property. I could see it in the distance like a lost boat at sea.

"You see," he continued. "I've been wanting to talk to you about your father, Eli. He hasn't been working or paying his rent, you know. I've warned him more than once that y'all are going to get kicked off the property if something doesn't change, but he won't listen to me. Every day it's the same thing. Splitting firewood or just pissing around in that shed behind y'all's house.

"Maybe if you talk to him, Eli. Tell him you're worried about losing your house or something—maybe that will motivate him. I just don't know what else to do."

I still didn't say anything. Even though I liked Mr. Tally, my parents had always taught me to not trust anyone in a position of authority. That we were on our own as a family, and our survival depended on our loyalty to one another.

Mr. Tally and I approached the house, and I could see the single floodlight that was bathing the yard a soft yellow. My dad was sitting on the porch. He didn't look up, though I know he had to have heard the four-wheeler's approach.

"All right," Mr. Tally said, not acknowledging my dad's presence, but looking back at me as I climbed from behind him and onto the grass. "Think about what I told you, young man."

"Yes, sir," I said. "I will."

As I walked across the dusty yard, I could see my dad sitting there on the porch, smoking a pipe and reading his Bible. The orange glow from the pipe pulsed in the dark as he inhaled the sweet-smelling smoke and then blew it back out. Then Mr. Tally drove away as I walked up the crooked porch steps to face my dad.

13

He was angry after I told him what Mr. Tally had said. "He shouldn't have told you that," he said. "It's none of your business what happens between me and him."

"Are we gonna lose our house?" I asked.

"You don't need to be worrying about that, son. We'll always have someplace to live. Your mother and I will take care of it."

I nodded but didn't say anything.

The next morning when I got up, I was happy to see my dad working by himself in the yard. He was building what looked like an animal cage of some kind, nailing a stack of two by fours and two by sixes together to form a rectangle that stood on legs about four feet high.

My dad was sweating in the sun as he worked. It really was a welcomed sight for me though, especially after what Mr. Tally had said the night before. So I decided I would skip breakfast, go outside, and help him. My mother was still sleeping, so I slipped past her room and through the den, then outside into the bright and early morning.

As I approached my dad, I realized the cage he was building was likely going to be for more of Mr. Tally's rabbits. Mr. Tally had hundreds of them, it seemed, sitting in cages similar to the one my dad was working on, and he kept them all under an eave behind his barn. Mr. Tally bred these rabbits and sold them off and probably even ate some of them too, my dad had said; still, it seemed like he always needed more space to keep them in. I didn't know much about rabbits myself, just that they were in a great abundance there on the farm.

Mr. Tally had all kinds of different colors and breeds of those rabbits. Big ones, small ones. Some with odd deformities like missing eyes, lopped-off ears, crooked legs. There were tons of them—and they were constantly mating, eating, and covering the ground beneath their cages with thousands of tiny brown pellets that I would sometimes have to rake up into piles of old hay, throwing all of it into a compost for Mr. Tally's garden. He would usually pay me a couple of dollars to complete this chore, and even if he hadn't, I was just happy to have something to do.

"Good morning," I said when I got to where my dad was working. "Need any help with that?"

"Not just yet," he said. "But don't go too far. I'll probably need you to help me flip this frame over in a minute so I can nail on the mesh at the bottom."

"Okay," I said, sitting down in the dusty grass, watching him work.

He seemed strangely happy that morning, as if being productive and earning money for his family satisfied him in a way that nothing else could. I didn't understand why he didn't do it more often.

Either way, I was just glad to see my dad working again. And even though it wasn't much, little odd jobs like this always helped. I thought Mr. Tally was pretty generous in giving my dad the work, especially after what he had said to me the night before. I even started to wonder if he really needed the cage built at all, or if he had just thought up some random job to keep my dad busy, productive.

But I do know that when my dad worked, he did good work. He believed in doing a thing right. And this cage was no exception: the frame was built in a way that you could easily stand there and change out the rabbit's water or take out the sick rabbits if you needed to. In addition to carpentering the frame, my dad had already nailed on some door hinges and a small door, which you could unlatch from a hasp so that you could pull the rabbits out easily. He had also stapled some mesh wiring to the sides.

I was still sitting in the grass and watching my dad do all of this, waiting for him to need me, when I suddenly heard him yell in what sounded like pain. "Dammit," he said.

I didn't say anything at first, didn't do anything either. I was used to hearing my dad curse when he was working on something.

But then he said it again: "Dammit."

He still had his back to me, but now he had stopped hammering.

He wasn't moving. Just sitting still and facing the frame. Then he dropped the hammer. It fell into the dust and made a small cloud beside his boots.

"Eli, get up and come over here quick," he said. He still hadn't turned around. I hadn't realized yet that he was stuck that way, unable to turn his body away from the cage.

I stood up and walked over to where he was, then over to the side of the cage where I could see his straining, pain-reddened face. By then, his eyes were starting to roll up in his head, and I could see their whites surrounded by the red rims of flesh that encapsulated them. I looked down and saw that my dad's right hand was pressed tight against one of the two by fours, how a piece of the wire mesh lay bent down above it like a sheet of folded paper.

Then I saw dark blood coming down from his hand and steadily dripping over his hairy wrist; it soaked the sleeve of the flannel shirt he was wearing. I moved closer as he started to lean back, sway forward a bit, then lean back again. It was as though he were dancing, or drunk.

It looked as if he were going to fall down, but his hand was still pressed against one of the two by fours, keeping him in place. As I looked closer, I could see a long, rusty nail poking out from the back of his hand, holding him against the rabbit cage. He had somehow nailed his own hand to the two by four.

He looked up at me, dazed.

"What happened?" I said.

My dad focused his bloodshot eyes on me for a second, his head wavering on his shoulders like a bowling ball in a tray.

"I ran a nail through my damn hand," he said. "Go get your mother. Quick."

I stood there, trying to imagine how my dad could have possibly done that. He could be pretty careless at times, but I just couldn't wrap my mind around this.

"Hurry," he said, the shocked pain in his voice yanking me out of my reverie. I turned around and ran back to the house.

My mother was inside sitting at the kitchen counter by then, drinking tea and listening to music.

"Mom, Dad just had an accident," I told her between breaths, the screen door slamming shut against my back as I stood in the threshold. "I think he nailed his hand to that cage he's working on." The words sounded odd coming out of me, like I was acting out lines in a play.

"What?" My mother stood, the magazine she was looking at falling to her feet, its pages fluttering shut on the floor.

"He needs help," I said.

My mother sat back down. Her eyes darted across the counter, then back up at me. "What are we going to do, Eli?"

"I don't know. But we have to help him. Do something. Call Mr. Tally. 911."

My mother just sat there, stunned. She seemed so calm, but I could tell by her eyes that she was panicking. I looked over at the counter's surface and saw the opened bottle of pills next to her cup. They were for anxiety, she had told me once, but she had started taking them more and more frequently, it seemed, as her fights with my dad increased and the pressures of living alone out here on the farm built day after day. This morning she looked completely stoned on them.

She was frozen. I briefly thought about that comic strip I had drawn, the bad kid trying to give the younger child all those pills, how he had told them no, and how my mother had laughed at that. Now I knew why. I also knew that I would be on my own trying to help my dad.

I ran back out to the yard to where he stood leaning against the half-finished rabbit cage. He wasn't saying anything and his eyes were closed, but he opened them and looked at me as soon as he heard me coming.

"Where's your mother?" he said, leaning and wavering again as though he were about to faint. I put my hand on his back to hold him steady, to keep him from falling. I shuddered at the thought of him ripping free from the nail, what it would do to his hand if that happened.

Still he was losing what looked to be a good amount of blood. His skin was starting to turn pale.

"Mom wasn't inside," I lied. "I don't know where she is." I couldn't bring myself to tell him the truth.

Then he said, without seeming to think about it, "Then I need you to pick up that hammer off the ground and pull out this nail before I pass out. I'm losing a lot of blood right now."

I watched his eyes roll back again, his eyelids start to flutter, and so I bent down and picked up the hammer from where it lay in the dust. It was heavy. I had never held or used it before. I turned it over in my hand, thought about when my dad had made me use his hatchet to chop off that poor chicken's head.

"Hurry," he said. "Just take that claw on the end and hook it on the nail. Don't worry about my arm. Just grip it as best you can."

I did what he said, but hesitated when it came to pressing the wooden handle against his arm for the leverage I'd need to pull out the nail from his hand.

"Come on, son. Just press it against my forearm if you have to. Don't worry about hurting me. Just go." His pallor had gone almost completely white by then. "Hurry," he said again.

Using his arm for leverage like he told me to, I leaned into the hammer's handle with just enough force to pry the nail from the board. I could hear it creaking inside the wood as I eased it out, and then I heard my dad's skin popping as the nail finally slid loose, dangling from the claw of the hammer in a mess of blood and rust.

When his hand was freed, he fell down into the dust and looked at his palm, his fingers frozen in place like small branches on a dead tree. Then he eased back onto the ground and closed his eyes against the sun. He was breathing heavily, as if he'd just finished running around the perimeter of the farm.

"Are you okay?" I said.

"Yeah. Just let me sit here for a minute. Why don't you go inside and see if we have any hydrogen peroxide or some rubbing alcohol or something."

"You don't think you should go to the hospital?"

"They're not going to do anything. Probably'll want to know if I've had a tetanus shot recently, then charge us a thousand bucks. I really just need to clean out this hole and I'll be fine. Just go look, okay?"

"Okay."

He kept his eyes closed against the glare overhead and wiped at the sweat on his face with his shirtsleeve as I walked back inside to find something to pour in his wound. My mother was no longer sitting in the kitchen, but I could hear the music she was listening to coming from her bedroom. I went to the door and knocked.

"Mom?"

She didn't answer, but I heard the sheets moving as she shifted in the bed. I knew she could hear me through the door.

"Do we have any hydrogen peroxide or rubbing alcohol? Dad needs some."

"I'm trying to take a nap, Eli. Tell him to come look himself."

"He's really hurt, Mom. Can I just come in?"

She didn't answer me so I opened the door and walked in. The curtains were drawn shut, but my mother had the windows open, letting in what breeze was outside, catching the incense and whispering its smell of smoky lavender around the room. Everything in there had a dark green tint to it from the curtains; the fan wobbled and ticked on its loose base in the ceiling. Music trickled softly from the speaker on her little wooden turntable.

She looked at me from where she lay in the bed, then pulled the sheets up over her face as I walked past her and into the bathroom. When I opened the medicine cabinet to look for the peroxide, I caught a glimpse of my face in the mirror. My skin was flushed from being in the heat. Beads of sweat hung on my upper lip, and my hair was wet too.

I looked around the shelves, pushed aside pill bottles and tubes of ointment until I saw the rubbing alcohol toward the back of the cabinet. I picked it up, grabbed some cotton balls from under the sink, and then went through my mother's dark room again. She didn't say anything to me as I left. She was still under the sheets when I pulled the door shut. Then I went through the den and back outside.

When I got into the yard, my dad was still lying in the dirt next to the unfinished rabbit cage. "Dad?" I said. He had wrapped his hand in his flannel shirt and was holding it against his chest. He opened his eyes and looked up at me.

"Did you find it?" he said.

"Yeah. Here." I handed him the bottle.

"Did your mother ever get back from wherever she was?" I watched him unwrap his hand from the flannel shirt, then heard him suck at his teeth as he poured what remained in the bottle of alcohol into his wound. He looked up at me, his eyes squinting against the sun and the pain.

"I don't think she did," I lied again. "I didn't see her."

He just nodded. "Burns," he said.

I knew he would find my mother in the bed when he got in the house, but I had hoped he wouldn't say anything to her, or that he would think she had come inside after all of this had happened. Ever since their fight over the chicken parts in the kitchen that afternoon, I had started making more of an effort to divert their attention from one another, to keep the peace between them. And so I knew that when he got in the house with his bandaged-up hand that I'd have to make up some excuse for my mom's presence, explain why she hadn't come out to help him. I'd just have to worry about that later, though.

"Well, don't tell her about this," he said. "Okay? What she doesn't know won't kill her." He smiled at me when he said this, and I thought then that everything might actually be okay.

"Yes, sir," I said. We sat there for a few minutes as my dad caught his breath, then we both stood and tried to finish up the frame of the cage. He told me where to hold the boards as he nailed them up with his good hand, his other one still wrapped in flannel and hanging limply at his side.

At some point later in the day, my mother came outside and brisked past us on her way to the open field, which was just beyond Mr. Tally's house and barn. She was smoking a clove cigarette, a little skinny brown one hanging from her lip as carelessly as a blade of grass in the breeze.

"Looks good," she said, nodding her chin at the rabbit cage. She didn't say anything about me coming inside earlier, about Dad being hurt, his bandaged hand.

"Thanks," he said. "Where've you been all day, Rebekah? And where are you going now?"

My mother ignored the first question, but in response to the second one, she said, wistfully, "Oh, nowhere. Just walking. This sunlight over the field is just too beautiful to not experience."

"Okay, dear," my dad said, looking at me. Smiling. "Have fun." Then he winked at me. Either he had decided not to confront my mother about where she had been when he needed her help or he had just made up his mind to ignore it this time. Whatever his thought process was, I was just glad there wasn't a fight. Maybe he was just content enough to be working and busy for a change.

I reached up to hold the rest of the wire mesh so that he could finish nailing it in. We needed it done before dark so that we could help Mr. Tally put it under the tin eave at the back of his barn and then help him put the rabbits inside of it. To give Mr. Tally a sense that we had earned our keep that day.

But a few hours later, when we finally brought the cage to him, Mr. Tally wasn't happy with the work we had done.

"John, what is this?" he said. "I can't use this. It's too small."

"I can build another one just like it. I just thought two or three smaller ones would be better. So you can put them in different places."

"Look, John, I appreciate what you did, I really do, but I asked for a specific dimension on this cage for a reason. I don't have room behind the barn to keep lining up cages like this. I just can't accept it. Not this way. Either rebuild it the way I asked, or I add the cost of materials, plus the time, to what you already owe me for rent. And since I haven't seen you go to work anywhere else in over two weeks, I know you don't have any money to pay me. So what's it gonna be?"

My dad looked humiliated. He ignored Mr. Tally, just told me to get back in the truck and wait for him. Then he closed the tailgate on the failed rabbit cage where it sat in the truckbed like a pile of garbage bags filled with rotting food, and he walked around to the driver's side of the cab. I knew that this probably wouldn't have been as hard on him had I not been there, listening. I wished I'd just stayed back at our house.

"What happened to you, by the way? Can you even work like that?" Mr. Tally asked, looking down at my dad's bandaged hand, which was still wrapped in a swatch of bloody flannel that he had ripped from the side of his shirt. The blood had dried and the cloth was now crusted-over and brown.

My dad didn't bother answering that question either. He just climbed into the sweaty cab, the seat creaking under him as he pulled the rusty door shut with his good hand, reaching across his chest to do so. The old door protested on its hinges as it came closed and I sat there, waiting to see what would happen. But nothing did.

Then he started the engine and pulled away from Mr. Tally's barn, leaving him standing in a blooming cloud of dust.

14

The next day I woke up to my dad and Mr. Tally yelling at each other out in the yard. I heard Mr. Tally say that we had to leave the property by the end of the week.

"Where are we supposed to go?" my dad said. "I have a wife and a young boy to think about."

"Well, you've certainly had plenty of time to think about them, John. I can't keep doing this. I'm not a charity worker. I have a business to maintain here. You simply have to leave."

My dad turned his back on Mr. Tally, and from where I was watching through the window, I saw Mr. Tally climb back onto his four-wheeler and start to pull off. Before he left, though, he stopped and said, "The end of the week, John. After that, I'm calling the sheriff."

My dad didn't say anything, just walked up to the porch, sat down in one of Mr. Tally's rocking chairs that had been there since we first moved in, lit a cigar, then started reading his Bible. It was as though nothing had happened.

A little while later, I could hear him walking into the house. I heard the screen door smack shut behind him, then my mother asking him what we were going to do.

"I don't know, Rebekah. Just let me think for a little while, okay? I'll figure something out."

Then I heard him walk back outside and onto the porch.

My mother was in the kitchen crying now, but I just stayed in my room. I knew it was best to not try to console her when she was like that. She had her pills and I was sure that those were probably far better than anything I could offer her: her eyes glassing over in watery peace, the lilt of a smile nudging at her cheeks as though someone were whispering a joke into her ear, something no one else but her could understand.

I looked out of my window and saw my dad walking in the yard. He was pacing around, not really doing anything, but I could tell he was frustrated by how quickly he was moving, as though his legs were scythes and he was slicing through the grass with them as he walked and paced, walked and paced. Then he went up to one of the little trash trees that littered our yard, and I watched as he punched at the tree again and again with his one good hand.

The bark was white—chipped tan or yellow in some places—and after a few minutes, I could see the skinny tree trunk as it became stained with his dark blood. His knuckles were cracking, his fingers bending at weird angles, yet still he kept punching away. I could hear the soft thumps, like a heart beating through the rubber tube of a stethoscope. I wondered how he would be able to do anything if both of his hands were hurt.

After he had worn himself into exhaustion, he fell to the ground at the bole of the tree. I watched him as he sat there and wept. He couldn't have known I was watching him; otherwise, he would've never done what he was doing then, and I felt almost ashamed to be witnessing this. My dad, crying. It was almost like watching my world slowly come to an end.

The only other time I had seen him anywhere near being like that was one time when he had accidentally hit a dog with his truck. I remember that the dog wasn't dead though, so my dad had to get out of the cab and shoot it. To put it out of its misery, he had told me. My mother wasn't with us that day, but I remember him telling her about it later. How I had seen the small globules of tears pooling underneath his eyes before he swiped them off with the back of his greasy hand. It was the only other time that I had seen my dad cry, or even come close to it.

I can still remember, too, watching him through the side-view mirror as he walked around the back of the truck with the shotgun he had slid out from the wooden rack in the cab. How the black barrel rubbed against his jeans as the dog's tail twitched against the dry grass, waiting. How its glassy eye followed my dad's slow and deliberate movements as though it knew what was about to happen to it.

I didn't want to watch, but I couldn't look away either. The sun glared down and it was almost as though I could see the shot before I heard it. The spray of blood and gravel and dirt, the way the poor animal's body jerked up against my dad's boots. I jumped. And it seemed as though the whole cab shook.

Before I looked away—not wanting my dad to know that I had seen what he had done—I watched as he cracked open the barrel and ejected the red plastic shell from the chamber. How it smoked as it spilled out onto the ground. Then he placed the shotgun in the bed of the truck instead of putting it back in the cab, climbed in, and pulled back out onto the highway. Neither one of us had said anything to each other, but I could tell by his eyes that he had been crying.

My mother weeping in the kitchen was one thing, something I'd seen and heard many times before, but seeing my dad like that— leaning against a tree in the back yard, sobbing into his bloody and bandaged hands—was almost too much for me to bear. So I just stared at him out of my dusty window and worried about what was going to happen to us. It was all I could do.

15

Later that evening, as I was lying in bed, my dad knocked on my door. He came into my room before I could answer him.

I sat up.

"Eli," he said, "I need you to come with me."

"Where?"

"I just need your help for a little while," he said. "Get dressed and meet me on the porch, okay?"

I didn't like the look in his eyes. He looked desperate, wild. Angry. I wasn't sure what he was thinking, but I was more afraid of not meeting him outside than I was of actually going with him, so I went out of my room, down the hall, and toward the den. I stopped first at my mother's room and put my ear against the closed door.

I could hear my mother in there listening to her old records again. I imagined her lying on top of the cool sheets in the gloom, her hair flowing loose against the pillows under her head, some lavender-scented incense burning on the nightstand beside her.

Living out here on another man's farm in the middle of nowhere with no friends or family to visit us, I couldn't blame her for behaving this way. If my mother needed pills and all that soft, flowery music in order to cope with her reality, then so be it. Especially if it meant that my life would be a little bit easier too—her being cloistered away like that meant I became invisible to her, which was usually a good thing.

I listened at the door for a minute longer, then walked out of the house to help my dad, who was waiting in the yard. Even in the dying sun, which was slowly slinking down behind the tree line, I could see that unpredictable look in his eyes. It frightened me not knowing what he had on his mind.

"Come on, Eli," he said. "Let's go."

I followed him, but I was still hopeful. Maybe he was going to ask me to start helping him pack our stuff. Maybe he wanted to take a drive into town to start looking for a new house to rent. Maybe he was going to try to have one more discussion with Mr. Tally, try to buy us some more time, or get him to change his mind altogether about us being evicted.

But all of my hope disintegrated when my dad handed me a knife. The same knife I had won at the fair, the same one he had taken from me and hidden away somewhere. I was relieved to see that he hadn't thrown it away, but now I was starting to worry about what he was going to ask me to do with it. The hand he had been punching the tree with earlier seemed better now, as his fingers were wrapped tightly around the hilt when he passed it to me. His other hand was still wrapped up in the strip of flannel.

"Take this and put it underneath your shirt," he said.

"Dad, I thought—" I really didn't know what I thought, what I was about to say but, either way, he stopped me before I could finish.

"Come on," he said. "Follow me."

He crouched down a bit and started sneaking across our small yard toward the fence line. I did as he told me and followed him. We were like two thieves moving in the twilight. When we got to the barbed wire, he lifted the top strand with his hand, then pushed down on the lower strand with his boot. "Go on," he said. "I'll be right behind you."

By now, it was as though I were moving in a fog, like when my parents and I went canoeing on the Bogue Chitto River one morning, just as the sun was beginning to rise. A thick plume of white mist hung over the still waters, and the glare coming off of the river's surface made everything feel as though it were moving slowly, like we were paddling through a wall of cotton stretched from one side of the river to the next, its white strands pulled taut like spiderwebs.

I remember that I kept thinking we were going to come out the other end of a cave, that we'd be transported to a different part of the country, or the world, or another planet even. And that was how I felt now as I stood looking at my dad parting the strands of barbed wire for me to go through, like Moses parting the Red Sea. I knew that once I crossed that line, though, something irrevocable was going to happen, something I would be helpless to stop once I started it into motion. But it was too late to turn back.

"Come on," he said. "Go."

So I did.

I went through the barbed wire, stepping in the wet grass on the other side and then waiting for him to come through behind me. The cows stood like large boulders in the pasture as we slunk across it, the two of us, and I could almost feel their eyes on us as we moved. In the distance, I could see Mr. Tally's barn rising up from behind a crest in the field and I didn't need my dad to say anything to know what we were doing, where we were headed.

I felt at the hilt of the knife in my waistband and tried to parcel out what was happening to me. Was all of this my fault? Had I not sent in that comic, none of this would be happening right now. It seemed as though I had set something into motion that I was now powerless to stop.

"Don't worry, son," my dad was saying, "we're not going to hurt anyone, okay? We're just going to leave this selfish S.O.B. a message."

We were stopped at the tree line bordering Mr. Tally's barn now. It was mostly dark outside by then and I could see the warm yellow light emanating from his house, which was just across from where my dad and I stood.

We watched Mr. Tally's house for a few minutes, waiting for the dogs to stop barking, and then my dad told me to follow him to the barn. I hadn't seen him holding any matches or gasoline, so I was hopeful he hadn't planned to commit arson like in that short story my mother told me about, which she even tried to make me read once—the one about the boy who leaves his family after his dad burns down a bunch of people's barns. She had wanted me to read it as part of my homeschooling, she told me, but I couldn't make myself get through all those long paragraphs and flowery sentences. I lied and told my mother I liked it, though. And she seemed happy enough about that, whether she believed me or not.

Anyway, I still couldn't figure out what my dad had given me my knife back for, what he had planned for me to do with it. I would refuse to hurt any animals, if that's what he had been thinking, but for now I followed him to the side of the barn, where he stopped just outside of the reach of one of the floodlights that were attached to the eaves. I could hear the rabbits scurrying around in their cages back there, and I thought about the cage my dad had built earlier, and how he had hurt his hand doing it.

"Hand me that knife," he said, putting out his good hand so he could take it from me.

I pulled the sheath from my pants and handed the whole thing to him, case and all, the hilt pointed toward him and the blade aimed at my own chest. I still didn't understand why he had me hold onto the knife like that when he could've just as easily carried it himself. But then I realized that it must have been his way to test my faith in him, to force me to be complicit in whatever it was he was about to do. The line had been drawn now, and I had unwittingly chosen a side whether I liked it or not.

I watched him as he unsheathed the blade, crouched down beside one of Mr. Tally's four-wheelers, looked over his shoulder one last time, and then jammed the knife into one of the tires. The tire didn't pop like I had expected it would though, but instead the air just sort of leaked out from the gash that my dad made. The four-wheeler lobbed to one side as he slipped out the knife blade, then went around and did the same thing to the other three tires, one by one.

We walked around the barn and I watched in silence as he did the same thing to two more four-wheelers, Mr. Tally's farm truck, and then his tractor, whose tires proved the most difficult, as they didn't even look like rubber; they were so thick they looked as though they were made out of cement, and my dad had to work at the blade to get it into each of them and deflate the air.

I kept hoping he wouldn't ask me to slash one, but when I saw the look of near-joy on his face as he destroyed this man's property—this man who had been so generous to us, who had us to his house for dinner, even if only for that one time—I was pretty sure he would finish the work himself. There was a certain pleasure, it seemed, that he was getting from all of this.

The whole time I just watched Mr. Tally's house, praying the porchlight wouldn't flick on, the screen door swing open as he materialized on the back porch, his shotgun shouldered and pointing out to where we stood.

But then my dad was standing straight, this time putting the knife in its sheath and clipping it on his own belt. He had gotten what he wanted from me already. I didn't need to carry the knife anymore. I had done my part and now it was time to go back home. And even though it was my knife, it was clear he intended on keeping it. I would never tell anyone what I had helped my dad do that night. Not my mother. Not anyone. And I would also never see that knife again for a long time, the only thing that had ever truly felt like mine.

16

We were evicted the next day. The sheriff sat in his car in the driveway as we fit what we could in the back of my dad's pickup truck. Mr. Tally watched us from the fence line, never coming toward us, but I knew he had told the sheriff about the slashed tires, and that he knew my dad had done it. If it hadn't been for my mother and me, Mr. Tally probably would've had him arrested.

But he had mercy on us.

So we spent the next few weeks sleeping in the bed of my dad's truck, parked in a wooded area off of Highway 16, my mother staying doped up on her pills most of the time, my dad taking me into town during the day to find odd jobs so we could pay for food and gas for the truck. At night, we would all sit in the pickup's damp bed, my dad reading Scripture to us by flashlight, my mother snoring softly against the words. The only other light was from the stars overhead, blinking in the lavender sky as though the god my father was reading to us about was trying to give us a more tangible message for our lives, something we could actually learn from. But I was starting to have my doubts that would ever happen.

One morning my dad woke me up early so that we could go out and look for money again. He had filled out a few applications here and there, had done some odd jobs around town, but when it got to the point where someone asked for his Social Security number, he'd wad up the pages of the job application dramatically, tossing them back at the person who'd handed them to him, then he'd grab my arm and pull me outside.

On that morning, though, my dad shook me awake under the looming gray of a tentative dawn, the frogs still chirping somewhere off in the woods, the grasshoppers from the night before still buzzing an incessant drone.

I could smell the rain coming, the scent of petrichor on the air. My mother stirred in her sleeping bag beside me, then rolled over toward the wheel well, where she continued to sleep. I climbed out of the back of the truck, gentling the tailgate shut so I wouldn't wake her.

"Good morning," my dad said. He looked as though he hadn't slept at all the previous night, and his hair was wild and greasy. I could see the dark circles under his eyes, the stubble that was covering his cheeks. He was smiling, but I could tell he was tired, worried. There was also something in him that seemed excited by our new struggle, our will to survive. He was always talking about how God tested the faithful, and how we should welcome those tests with open arms. He said that he actually appreciated these chances the Lord gave us to prove our family was worthy of God's love, and that my mother and I should appreciate them too.

I sat on the bumper and put on my tennis shoes. They were torn and ratty and damp. I could hear my stomach growling as I worked on the wet laces. I was hungry. I hadn't eaten at all the day before. Still, I tried to ignore the pain in my stomach as I went over to where my dad had put some tepid water in an ice chest for washing up. I splashed it on my face to wake myself.

Despite the gray skies and the fact that it was mid-November, it was still and humid outside. Winter rarely touched Louisiana, and when it did, it usually wasn't until January or later. So that morning it still felt like summer. My skin itched from the mosquito bites and the gnats that ate away at me as I tried to sleep. I forced myself to ignore this too, just rubbed some of the stale water on my skin to cool the burn.

"So I was reading this morning," my dad was saying, "that the price of aluminum is skyrocketing right now. I thought it wouldn't be a bad idea if we tried to fill up these yard bags with some cans this morning, see about recycling them."

"Okay," I said, relieved by the prospect of making money, my dad having a goal in his head, something productive to do with our time.

He handed me two black plastic yard bags. I could tell they had been used before. There were tiny gashes and tears across both of them, and the red drawstring that you used to cinch them closed was gone. "Once we fill a couple of these up," he said, "we can take them to this recycling place I saw down the road the other day."

I didn't answer, just looked at the bags in my hands, then looked up at the gray sky. My dad's eyes followed mine and as if reading my thoughts, he said, "If we start now, we can beat the rain. Come on."

His mood seemed upbeat, but I could tell it was forced. My mother made him feel guilty for getting us evicted from Mr. Tally's farm, and at night when they thought I was asleep, I could hear her telling him that CPS would take me away from them if we didn't find a place to live soon. We were homeless, she'd say. I wasn't in school, and we were starving. She told him these things again and again. My dad would just say, "I know. I'm trying."

Then they would fight quietly for a good hour or so before my mother found her way into the bed of the truck, where she would zip her body up into a moldy sleeping bag and sob herself to sleep. For several hours after that, I could hear my dad pacing around in the woods near our dying campfire, branches breaking beneath his footfall as he mumbled incoherently under his breath.

17

We walked alongside the highway, scouring the ditches for cans, picking up half-empty Budweisers and Coca-Colas, dumping out what liquid remained in them and then tossing the empty cans into our bags.

My dad stayed on one side of the road and I was on the other, the traffic coming toward me so that I could have enough time to see it and jump away should one of those speeding cars veer off onto the shoulder. My dad kept his back to the traffic, walking up the right side of the highway, plucking cans from the ditch and from the narrow slope of gravel that shouldered the road.

Within an hour, my dad had two large bags filled with sticky, dirty cans, draping the bags over his back like a vagrant Santa Claus, each one bumping against the backs of his legs as he walked.

The sky was almost completely gray by then—and getting darker with each passing minute. You could hear the thunder off in the distance. At any second, I knew, those clouds would open up and dump everything they had on us. If things could get any worse, I was convinced they would.

I had only one of my bags filled up, and some of the cans kept falling out from a tear in the plastic, making the hole bigger each time. I stopped and put the bag down next to the ditch. My dad was coming across the highway now, looking at me as he made his way over the cracked asphalt.

When he got to my side of the road, he put his bags down in the tall wispy weeds that were growing in the ditch. A breeze stirred the long grass around our calves. "Well," he said. "This should be good for now. That recycling place I was telling you about is right up the road. I think if we get there and weigh out with these three bags, we'll have enough to put a little gas in the truck, get a couple of sandwiches from the gas station. What do you think?"

"That sounds good," I said, trying to sound positive, if only for his sake.

"Great," he said. Then he looked up at the roiling sky as if he were trying to divine some meaning beyond the obvious portent of rain. He picked up all three bags. "Let's go," he said, leaving me to walk behind him, empty-handed.

When we got to the road that the recycling center was on, the rain finally started coming down, but not quite on us just yet. It was still off in the distance, but you could hear it in the woods as it came in angry sheets against the trees and the deadfall there. It was headed right for us, and there was nothing we could do but keep walking into the direction it was coming from.

The recycling center was at the end of a gravel road, surrounded by a fifteen-foot-high metal privacy fence. It was a large tin building that was in the middle of myriad stacked bales of crushed aluminum, dead cars, and old appliances, rusted out and with doors hanging on a solitary, squeaking hinge. The rain beating down on the metal sounded like machine gun fire, and I could see the two men who must've worked there standing under the tin shed and trying to talk to one another over the din. They watched us through a veil of rain and their own gray cigarette smoke as we approached them.

"How can we help you gentlemen?" one of them said, not moving from under the shelter of the tin roof, raising his voice over the noise.

My dad and I dropped our bags on the wet dirt, the rain immediately puddling in the creases of the bags, hitting the aluminum inside and adding to the overall racket. We walked under the shelter.

The floor inside was made up of packed dirt and there were loose cans scattered about, more old appliances, a forklift parked in a dark corner with a tight bale of crushed metal hoisted above its cab. A thin dog was tied to a rope that depended from one of the overhead beams, its tail thumping softly on the dirt. A couple of flies skittered about its water bowl as the dog puffed warm gusts of dusty air onto the ground beneath its dirty paws.

"You buy aluminum cans?" my dad asked one of the men.

"Yes, sir." The man looked out at the rain, then pitched the stub of his cigarette into it. "We pay eighty-five cents a pound. I reckon one of them bags probably weighs about five pounds, give or take. You're lookin' at a about twelve bucks, I'm figurin'."

"All right," my dad said. I could tell he was disappointed by the way his head hung slack, but I could also see his jaw working, as though he were calculating how far he could stretch that little bit of money on gas. Some food. All that time in the heat, walking through the ditch—not to mention that we still had to trudge all the way back to our truck in this rain—just for twelve dollars. But we were desperate and hungry. It would have to do.

"Why don't y'all bring them bags in and Darryl here can dump 'em on the scale for ya? See what you got."

"Okay," my dad said. "Eli, grab yours and I'll get these two."

"Yes, sir," I said.

My dad and I stepped back out into the sheet of rain, picked up our bags, and brought them into the shed. The man who had been smoking the cigarette when we came up had walked over to a wooden desk and was shuffling through some papers. Then he sat down and started pressing buttons on an adding machine. I couldn't hear the otherwise loud keys over the noise of the rain overhead, but I watched him as he worked out some figures that seemed to irritate him. He reached over and grabbed his pack of cigarettes, pulled one out, and put it in his mouth. The cigarette must've gotten wet, or was damp, because it sort of drooped down toward the man's chin, and it took at least six clicks of his lighter to get it lit. After he blew out a thick puff of gray air, he turned around and started marking something on a greasy Chevrolet calendar that had a picture of a woman in an American-flag bikini on it. She was posing next to a blue-and-white muscle car, its hood shiny and new, the sun glinting off the metallic paint like fingers of bright light reaching down from the sky. My dad would've said this was Satanic.

I watched as the junkman turned from his calendar and clicked on a small radio that was hanging from an orange bungee cord against the wall, though I doubted he could hear what came from its tinny speakers—with the rain and the thunder outside pounding against the tin roof like gravel falling from the sky.

I continued to watch him as he leaned over and poured some dark black coffee from a stained Mr. Coffee percolator and then into a mug that said "America: Love It or Leave It" with a yellowed American flag emblazoned on its side.

There was also a small plastic Christmas tree balancing just at the corner of his cluttered desk. It looked as though it could topple over at any second and at the slightest movement. The tree was draped with silver tinsel and a few sporadic blinking lights. I stared at it, watched the lights blink and flicker.

My parents didn't believe in celebrating Christmas. They said it was a pagan holiday. And because of that, I had never believed in Santa Claus or had experienced the magic of that particular time of year like most children did.

That pathetic little tree on the junkman's desk reminded me of the one year my mom was actually able to persuade my dad to get a tree and to celebrate the holiday like regular people. How we had walked out into the woods behind the house we were renting then, the three of us, and how my mother and I watched as my dad used an axe to chop down a gaunt pine. We dragged it back to our house and I remember helping my mom string popcorn onto a piece of thread and how we then wound it all around the sorry branches like wires on the inside of a building.

Still it was magical, and it had almost made me believe that things could for once be special in my family.

"So what do you want for Christmas this year, Eli?" my mother had asked me when we finished decorating the tree. We had used pine cones for ornaments, the strings of popcorn, and some drawings my mother had cut out from one of the encyclopedias we had.

I didn't know what to say: I was seven years old then and we had never celebrated Christmas before. When I had asked my parents about it some years before that, they told me that Christmas was a corporate holiday intended to make big business bigger and rich men richer. We were suckers if we participated, they had said.

They told me about the "myth" of Santa Claus, the story's pagan roots, and how they were afraid that if they let me in on this little lie, even just for fun, I would be susceptible to even more lies from our corrupt culture, the opiates used to sedate the masses with false joy and hope. We were all better off just sticking to the truth one hundred percent of the time, they had said.

But now here my mom and I were, decorating a Christmas tree, listening to her records, and she was asking me what I wanted for a Christmas present.

"I don't know," I said. "I thought you didn't believe in Christmas."

"Of course we believe in it, Eli—as in the day that celebrates the birth of Christ. We just don't believe in participating in the corporate sham that it's become in America."

"Oh."

"But one year of going along with the masses won't kill us, will it?"

"I guess not," I said, shrugging my shoulders.

"So, if you could ask for anything for Christmas this year," she said, her voice soft and sweet, "what would it be?"

"I don't know. Maybe a tent so I could sleep outside."

"That's a good present. Well, maybe Santa will bring it to you. Have you been a good boy?"

"Mom. Come on. I know all about that."

"Well, I know you do, Eli. But there's nothing wrong with pretending a little, is there?"

She patted the top of my head and pulled me closer to her. I could smell her skin and clothes—the soap she bathed with and the detergent she had scrubbed into her shirt. Then she stepped back and looked at our Christmas tree.

"What do you say we get some lights and put them on it too?" she said. "Wouldn't that be nice?"

"I don't know," I said. "I guess."

"Of course it would," she said.

So we rode our bikes down the road to a thrift store where my mother let me pick out some candy, a slingshot, and a single strand of Christmas lights. The lights weren't in their original packaging, but mostly all of them worked—and that was enough to make me happy.

On Christmas morning that year, I could hear my dad already awake and in the kitchen. It sounded as though he were washing dishes and humming to himself above the almost-peaceful clatter of glass and silverware and water.

I stumbled out of my bed and crept down the hallway so I wouldn't wake my mother. Then I went into the den. Under the tree were a couple of boxes, one or two of them wrapped with shiny aluminum foil, one with a sheet of faded construction paper, another with some newspaper—and all of them tied off with a length of brown twine from the shed. Even though I didn't believe anyone other than my parents had placed those small boxes there, wrapped them like that, it was still a magical feeling seeing those presents: things that weren't there the night before when I had gone to sleep.

I looked over from where I was standing and saw my dad in front of the sink, a cloud of steam from the dishes rising up from the hot water as he scrubbed them and placed them one by one on the drainboard to dry. He was still humming softly under his breath until he saw me. Then he stopped, clicking off the little radio on the windowsill. He shut off the faucet.

"Good morning, Eli," he said. "Merry Christmas."

"Merry Christmas, Dad," I said. I was aware that this was the first time in my life that I had uttered those words, that I had heard them uttered to me. Even at seven years old, it wasn't lost on me how odd it all felt.

"When your mother wakes up," he said, "we can open these presents."

He seemed to be in a lighter mood for a change. Usually he was so serious and grim, talking about Scripture or the end of the world, all the horrible things our society was doing to our brains— the chemicals in our food, television, rock-and-roll music, the ever-expanding federal government, who wanted nothing but to erode our personal freedoms.

But that morning he didn't mention any of those things. It was Christmas.

Around 10:30 when my mother finally woke up, I heard her stumbling around in the hallway before making her way into the den where my dad and I were waiting. He was reading his Bible and I was on the floor filling in a used coloring book that had missing pages and mostly colored-in pictures, the nubs of crayon fanned out on the floor before me like cigarette butts in an ashtray.

I looked up at the sound of her coming into the den. She looked disheveled and tired still.

"Good morning, Mom. Merry Christmas," I told her.

My mother didn't answer me, just looked across the room. Her eyes were puffy and her nightgown was wrinkled and hanging off her shoulders. Her pale skin underneath. My dad looked up at her from his Bible.

"Good morning," he said. "Everything okay?"

Just then my mother turned toward my dad, her eyes sharp now, her mouth no longer slack with sleep but tight and angry.

"Why in the fuck would you ask me that?" She said this slowly, as if each word were being pushed up one by one from the deepest part of her body.

"Leave it to you to ruin Christmas, John. How dare you ask me that? How dare you!"

My dad closed his Bible and started to get up from where he was sitting in the rocking chair. "Eli, why don't you go outside on the porch for a minute while I talk to your mother," he said.

I started to stand, but then my mother stopped me. "You don't need to go outside, sweetheart. It's Christmas morning. We're going to have a beautiful time today." Her voice was high pitched now and she was emphasizing words that didn't make sense. I could tell she was being sarcastic, but I wasn't sure why, or what was even going on. Something seemed to have come unhinged in her overnight. I didn't know what was happening.

My mother walked over to the tree that she and I had just decorated the day before. "Here," she said. "Let's open our presents. Let's see. Here's one for you, Eli. And another one for you. And here's one from me to your father." All the while her voice was lilting in a way that may have been mistaken for kindness had a stranger been listening, but I could tell my mother was infuriated. I just didn't understand why.

She was still holding the present for my dad, smiling strangely and looking out the window, through which a large cylinder of light was pouring in and covering her, the motes of dust floating around her as though it were snow.

Then she threw the box at my dad. It hit him in the face, then fell onto his lap and rolled onto the floor beside his feet. "Dammit, Rebekah," he said. "Calm down."

"No, you calm down! I can't take this anymore!"

My dad looked at me. "Eli, go outside," he said calmly. Too calmly, I thought, considering the state my mother was working herself into.

I got up and went to the front door and opened it, this time my mother not so much as noticing me leave. I walked out to the front porch and then into the yard. It was cool outside and I was still in my pajamas but I tried to get far enough away from the house so I couldn't hear my parents screaming. It was futile though.

"You never do anything right, John!" My mother's voice sliced through the closed windows. "You ruined Christmas! It's just one day out of the year. One we never even celebrate. And the one time we try, you ruin it!"

I couldn't hear my dad's response, but I figured he must have been saying something back to her in his calm and calculated way since my mother had actually stopped yelling for a moment. Then after a minute she picked back up:

"I'm done," she said, her voice quavering. "You can take your present and throw it away for all I care. Eli's too! I knew this was a bad idea!"

I started to run away from the house and toward the woods. Then I heard the front door open and close. I turned back and could see my dad ambling over the porch and out into the yard. He put his hand over his eyes to block out the glare from the sun, then he called out to me:

"Eli! Oh, Eli!"

I didn't answer him. Instead, I started walking back to the yard so that he could see I was still there. I still had no idea what had triggered my mother's behavior. She had been completely fine the day before.

When we met in the yard, my dad didn't say anything about

what had just happened. He was clutching his Bible at his side and asked if I wanted to read with him.

All I could manage was a halfhearted, "Okay."

So we sat down and I watched as my dad opened the book to Genesis, Chapter One, Verse One, and started to read: "In the beginning God created the heaven and the earth," he said, though I could tell he was distracted. He kept looking back at the door, as if my mother might emerge. But she must have gone back into her room because everything inside the house was quiet again, like it had been when I first woke up that morning.

18

A growl of thunder outside startled me, and I looked up from the junkman's Christmas tree and then over at my dad, who seemed slightly uncomfortable standing in the middle of this large shed and among the scattered piles of crushed aluminum cans—some of them baled and stacked inside of small chicken wire fences, the rain pelting the metal roof overhead. My dad scraped the tips of his boots in the dust, his head down, hands in his pockets.

"Why don't y'all bring them bags over here so I can dump 'em on the scale," the other man, Darryl, finally said over the noise.

"You just put the whole bag on there, right?" my dad said.

"No, sir. We dump all the cans out. Make sure you didn't weight them bags down with rocks or anything." Darryl smiled. Winked at me as he said this, but my dad looked serious and worried. He didn't say anything. Just stood there holding the bags in his hands.

We walked over to where Darryl was standing on a raised platform next to the scale, a broom leaning against his leg. I watched as he took a pack of cigarettes from his pocket and put one in his mouth. Lit it. Then my dad passed him one of the bags and Darryl grabbed it and uncinched the top, slowly pouring the cans onto the scale and then spreading them out with the broom. I watched the scale as it jerked and ticked.

Darryl called out some numbers to the junkman, who was still sitting at his desk at the far end of the shed, smoking and writing on a large yellow legal pad. The pages in it looked damp and wrinkled, like an old map. Then Darryl swept the cans from off the scale and into a small rectangle made out of chicken wire. He looked at me, noticed me watching him. "We'll crush 'em all later," he said. "You can watch, if you want."

I didn't say anything.

The edges of the cans winked shards of light from the narrow fluorescent bulbs that were suspended from the wooden rafters.

Then Darryl looked back to my dad. "Go 'head and hand me one of them otherns," he said. But my dad just stood there for a second, biting his bottom lip. I couldn't tell why he seemed so apprehensive.

He put down the bag he was holding and turned to me. "Why don't you hand me yours first, Eli?" he said. "I didn't know he was gonna empty 'em out like this first."

"Okay," I said, still not understanding why it mattered. So I just hefted my bag up and passed it to my dad, who then handed it to Darryl. He took it in his gloved hand and then did the same thing with my bag that he had done with my dad's. Called out another number to the junkman, who scribbled it all down in his pad, pressed a few keys on the adding machine on his desk.

When Darryl looked back to my dad for the last bag, my dad ignored him at first. Stood there fidgeting in the dirt, the sound of rain overhead seeming to emphasize his own nervous energy.

"You wanna hand me that last one there, bud?" he said.

"Look," my dad said, moving closer to Darryl but still not passing him the bag. "We're really hungry. Me and my boy here. My wife's sleeping right now in the back of my pickup truck out in the woods. We don't have anywhere to stay."

Darryl just stared down at my dad from where he stood next to the scale, a cigarette hanging from his lip, the broom still at his side. He shifted his weight on the platform, appearing to puzzle out what my dad was trying to tell him.

"I understand, man," he finally said. "Don't worry about it. We'll give you some money for these cans. I know it ain't much but at least it's somethin'." He smiled.

By now the junkman was coming over from where he had been working at his desk. It was as though he could sense that something was wrong. Darryl just pitched his cigarette onto the dirt, looked away nervously. I still didn't know what was going on.

"Y'all don't got no rocks in there or anything, do you?" the junkman said.

My dad didn't say anything.

"Now you should know that I don't abide folks who try to cheat me. I run an honest business here and I expect everyone else to do the same."

"We'll just go then," my dad said. "We don't want to cause any trouble."

"I'm afraid you already did," the junkman said, yanking the last remaining yard bag from my dad's closed fist. "I knew there was somethin' suspicious about you. I could tell as soon as you came in here. Walkin' up through the rain like that. See, Darryl," he said. "I told you I could read people."

Darryl continued to look away, as though he were embarrassed by this whole exchange.

"So what you got in here? Is it rocks? Is that it? Huh?"

My dad was quiet.

The junkman looked at me, shook his head as though I, too, were in on whatever was happening. Then he flipped the bag upside down and dumped its contents onto the dirt, nudging over the pile of cans with his boot until they were in a single layer on the ground.

It seemed as though we all saw it at once—what was at the bottom of the bag, making it weigh more than what it should have weighed. It was a baseball, and my dad must have put it there. All his talk about lying and cheating, the mortal sins, and now he was guilty of the same thing he was always preaching to me about. But I wondered if the lie was okay if it was to help your family. Part of me wondered if what my dad had done was honorable—he was just trying to take care of us. In that moment I actually think I loved him for that.

The junkman bent over and picked up the baseball. "Here's the culprit," he said. "Pretty creative, huh, Darryl?" But Darryl was still looking in the other direction and didn't say anything.

It didn't seem to matter. The junkman kept talking to my dad, his voice rising over the rain and with a heated anger now too. "Most folks just stick rocks in their bags," he was saying. "Think we won't see 'em. Had a few people try to weigh in cans that were still full of soda. Seen a brick once. A crowbar. But never a baseball. I think I might have to keep this one in my hall-of-fame. What do you say, Darryl? You think we should keep it?"

Still he said nothing in response.

The junkman tossed the ball up in the air for added effect. "Unbelievable," he said. Then he said it again. "Unbelievable."

"You see," the junkman said, looking back to my dad again, "it's this sort of thing that can really ruin a man's trust." He shook his head, then tossed the ball underhanded at my dad, who caught it, surprisingly, and stared down at it in his hand as though he were a child being scolded by his parents. I had never seen him look like that before.

"And on second thought," the junkman was saying, "I think you should keep that baseball. Maybe it will remind you to be honest with folks from now on." I couldn't imagine the humiliation my dad must have felt, especially with me standing there. Having his work rejected by Mr. Tally in front of me was one thing, but having me witness his being accused of lying must have been unbearable for him. He didn't say a word. Neither did I.

Then the junkman put his hands in his pockets, a gesture that seemed to suggest some kind of finality, that this conversation with my dad was over.

"Darryl?" he said. "We're gonna keep all these cans too, okay? For our troubles."

"Yes, sir," Darryl said, keeping his eyes on the ground, refusing to look at me or my dad now. I could tell he was ashamed to be a part of this transaction.

"Good," the junkman said. "Now y'all get the hell out of my place of business."

My dad looked at me. "Come on, son," he said. "Let's go."

We started walking toward the large opening at the front of the recycling shed, which seemed to be curtained off by a sheet of white rain outside. The sun had started to come out from behind a scud of gray clouds though, and it made everything hazy and bright. The heavy drops of rain splashed in the mud at the entrance to the shed. But you could still hardly hear anything over the din of it against the metal roof.

My dad was still holding the baseball. I could see it in his hand. It was tanned slightly, with red stitching holding the two flaps of cracked leather to its kapok core. I wondered where he had even gotten it, but guessed he had just picked it up from the side of the road earlier and had stuffed it into his bag with the cans.

He didn't look back to see if I was following him out of the shed or not, and at first I wasn't. Instead, I stood there and just watched the rain pummel the earth into muddy rivulets and oil-skeined puddles outside. The glaze of it on the dead appliances. I listened to the occasional drum of thunder coming from the clouds overhead, the rain jabbing the tin roof and pouring down from the eaves.

The junkman had gone back to his desk already, was using a stub of pencil to write something else in his ledger. Then the telephone rang and he picked up its greasy black receiver. Held it close to his face. He put the pencil down among the clutter and plugged his ear with his finger, seemed to strain to hear what the caller was saying over the noise from outside.

That was when the man Darryl came up behind me and said something so softly that I could barely make it out. "Do y'all go to church?" he said. His eyes were moving back and forth from me to his boss. He seemed nervous to be talking to me. As though he knew he'd get in trouble for it, but had to anyway.

Something told me not to turn around and face him directly, that this was supposed to be a private conversation. I chanced a look over at the junkman again, still at his desk, talking loudly into the phone, his stubbled, gray cheek brushing up against the receiver like sandpaper. He seemed to have already forgotten about my dad and me.

"No, sir," I said to Darryl. "I mean, at least not for a long time."

"Well, you should take this," he said.

I felt him slide a small piece of folded paper into my fingers. It was damp from the humidity and the rain but I didn't look at it then. Instead, I just held it in my hand and rubbed its crease along my palm.

"That has all the information you'll ever need in it," Darryl said from behind me. "Promise me you'll show it to your father later."

"Okay," I said. "I will."

The junkman was still on the phone, shuffling papers on his desk, yelling at whomever was on the other end of the line.

"Here," Darryl said. "Take this too." I felt him slide another piece of paper into my hand. "Don't tell your dad I gave this to you, but please just promise me you'll show him that tract. We can give you and your family shelter, food. The kind of nourishment you won't even know you were missing until you have it."

"Okay," I said again, stuffing everything Darryl had handed me into my back pocket.

"Now go," he said. "Before I get into more trouble than I'm already in."

I didn't know what else to say, so I just said, "Thank you," and walked out the large opening at the front of the shed and then into the rain and the sun and the still-thundering clouds. But they were starting to clear finally, and the rain was slackening.

My dad was already standing at the edge of the clearing, just near the fence line. He was waiting for me next to some junked-out cars, their glistening metal frames steaming now in the rain, the skinny boles of pine trees jutting out from the ground and turned black from dampness, a dark contrast to the white glare surrounding them.

"What were you doing in there?" he said. "I thought you were behind me."

"Sorry," I said. "I was just waiting for the rain to let up some."

"Well, come on. Your mother's probably worried about us. And we still have to figure out what to do about money."

"Yes, sir," I said.

We started walking down the gravel drive leading back to the highway, and as I followed behind my dad, staring at the arch of his back—which seemed to bend further under the weight of all that had just happened—I watched as he reached his arm over his shoulder and tossed the baseball into the woods. It landed in the mud and sunk partway in so that it protruded from the ground like an over-sized marble, or a single eye staring out from the wet earth.

Then he stopped. Looked back at me. The rain had finally ceased—almost suddenly, it seemed—and with the sun glaring white and hot onto him, little curtains of steam rising up from the gravel driveway, he said, "Don't worry, Eli." He grabbed my shoulders, looked at my face. "Okay? It's all going to be just fine," he said.

I felt my back pocket to make sure that everything Darryl had handed to me was still there. I wanted to know what it all was before I mentioned it to my parents. But I would have to wait until we got back to the truck to look at it.

"Yes, sir," I said.

"Good." My dad squeezed my shoulders. Tight. Then patted me on the head. "Let's go," he said.

We started walking side by side down the road, the gravel crunching under our shoes. A spine of tall grass in the middle of the lane separated the muddy wheel ruts on either side and I could see the mosquitoes and dragonflies alight on the wet, drooping blades. Water dripped from the branches on either side of us. The birds were already coming back out.

19

As we walked back to our truck in the woods, the road steaming beneath our shoes from the rain, I stayed a few steps behind my dad so that I could see what Darryl had handed to me in the recycling shed. I couldn't wait. I just had to know. So I reached into my back pocket and pulled out the wad of damp paper.

Folded up in my hand was a twenty-dollar bill. There was also a tract that had the same picture and writing as the one that the lady at the fair had handed to me. I had thrown that one away in the ditch as my dad and I left the fair that night, but here I was looking at it again: the same colorful wording, the same slightly unfocused picture of the man with the thick brown beard and long hair. His arms open, his face looking peacefully skyward. His eyes seemed to follow you as you moved the tract around in your hands.

Beneath his photograph, though, was slightly different wording from the other tract I had been given. The words were still italicized or bolded in what seemed strange places for emphasis. It said, "Come to **me**, all you who are *weary* and *burdened*, and I will give you **REST**.—Matthew 11:28." Then in a smaller font below that, but in red this time instead of yellow: "Sundays @ 10AM."

I didn't remember if the tract I had gotten last time had this information on it, but here it was, below the day and time of service: the name of the church, its address, and phone number. I'm sure it had been there on the other tract, but I just hadn't noticed it then. I hadn't needed to. Back then—just a couple of weeks ago—we had a place to live, had food to eat. And I had thrown that tract away in the ditch. Now we were homeless and near starving. And the words on the paper seemed more significant somehow.

The church, it said, was here in Angie, not far from where we were living in the woods in my dad's truck. It was called Light of His Way.

"Dad?" I said, stopping on the gravel shoulder of the road and putting the tract back into my jeans pocket. He stopped walking, turned around.

"What's wrong?"

"Nothing," I said. "I have some money." I didn't know how else to say it other than to just be direct and see how he reacted.

He looked at me. "What?"

"That man at the junkyard—Darryl—he gave me twenty bucks."

"He did?" My dad's face seemed to change, as though I had flicked on a switch, bathing the room it was in with warm soft light.

"Yeah," I said. "Maybe we can use it to buy some food."

"He gave you twenty dollars?"

"Yes, sir."

He stared at me for a while longer. I couldn't tell if he was going to make me walk all the way back to the junkyard and return the money, if he'd just snatch it from me and toss it on the highway for the passing cars to blow into the ditch, or if he'd agree that we should keep it, use it for the food we so desperately needed. "You're a good boy, Eli," was all he said, which gave me at least a little bit of hope.

I didn't say anything—I didn't know what to say—but my dad and I kept walking down the highway and into town where I thought we might at least spend some of that money to get some food to bring back to Mom. I decided I would wait to tell him about the tract.

20

When we finally got into Angie, my dad and I stopped at the John's Curb Market. He said we could get some food, something to drink. So we walked past the gas pumps and pickup trucks, which were parked in the pea-gravel-and-asphalt lot outside, the white sun overhead glaring down on us, the steam from this morning's rain rising up from the tin roof like a thin gauze of smoke. The metal freezers with the word ICE written over them flanked the opening of the store like sentinels.

John's Curb was a low orange building with a rusty tin roof and a single island of gas pumps out front. There was an old hitching rail on side of the store for the folks in town who still rode up on horseback. Which they did. More than once I saw tractors with Bush Hogs, riding lawnmowers, four-wheelers, and one time even a go-kart parked outside.

There was a sign just past the perimeter of the parking lot with a blinking arrow on top, which pointed toward the store, a few of its white light bulbs missing, and on the lower part of the sign, in black plastic lettering was the abbreviated name of the store, "John's," its phone number, and below that, the words: "Boudin, Busch Light, VHS Rent. Open 7 Days. 6A–10P."

I can remember going into the store sometimes with my dad after helping him on Mr. Tally's property and getting an IBC or a Barq's root beer—those cold, brown bottles with the raised lettering on them. How the cool glass felt in your hands. My dad said they were poison, of course, but every now and then he would relent and let me have one. Once he had even let me get a Slush Puppie from the large humming machine behind the counter. I can still remember devouring those little pebbles of ice coated with nectar syrup, how they got stuck in the straw and you had to just take the lid off and drink the rest of it out of the cup like water.

The store inside had oily concrete floors and there were two lethargic ceiling fans spinning overhead, their long pull-chains dangling from the dim light fixtures like kite tails. They wafted around the smells of fried chicken, cheeseburgers, boudin, and shrimp Po'boys, which were kept wrapped in aluminum foil and baking under orange heat lamps.

There was a long wooden picnic table in the middle of the place where the old men would sit in the mornings and talk about the weather, their Styrofoam cups of black coffee steaming up into their grizzled faces and spreading out under the bill of their green John Deere hats like smoke from a dying bonfire.

Two large freezers hummed along the back wall—their coils clicking as people opened and shut the coolers' glass doors to get beer, RC Colas, milk—that fresh gush of cold air that came out from them seeming to fill the entire store with a temporary coolness.

John's Curb also rented movies. There were several rickety shelves along the side wall lined with faded VHS or Betamax boxes. Horror movies or John Wayne films, things my parents would have never let me watch, even if we had a television set and a VCR. Or a den to keep them in. Still I liked to look at the boxes when we went in there: their sun-faded covers. Just imagining what those movies were about could be enough sometimes.

The tiny bell above the door clinked as we walked into the cool darkness of the store. For a moment, as the door swung open, I looked at its tinted glass, which was covered with signs announcing all the things for sale inside, the large Visa and Mastercard stickers, the pieces of paper with the words, "We Take Checks" and "No Shirt No Shoes No Service" written in black marker and taped to the glass. The now-bright sun caught on the door as we opened it and reflected a bright swath of light across us. It washed onto the stained concrete floor as we walked through the threshold.

When we got inside I looked up and all I could see were the aisles stocked with canned food, chips, beef jerky. I could smell the fried chicken and the potato logs baking under the heat lamps. My stomach growled.

The tiled ceiling in there was low and some of the tiles were water-stained and drooping, the insulation sticking out from the beams between them like tufts of dark yellow clown hair. A few dim and flickering fluorescent lights lit up the place, but save for that and the tinted sunlight that leaked in through the front door, it was dark inside and cavelike.

A small TV was sitting on the countertop and was playing some action movie where two guys who looked like cops were shooting at a bunch of other people, who shot back at them indiscriminately, the flashes from the muzzles of their guns filling the screen with dramatic white light. The picture looked faded and it flickered on and off as though something inside the television set was dying. The man behind the counter still stared at it, though, the light reflecting across his face and his eyes as though he were completely hypnotized by what was happening in the film.

Since it was still midmorning the store was pretty quiet. My dad nodded at the two men who were sitting at the picnic table not talking to each other, but who were also just watching the small television on the counter by the register. They nodded back and didn't say anything either, just kept smoking their cigarettes in silence, flicking the ashes into a black plastic ashtray in the middle of the table.

My dad and I walked down the narrow aisles, looking at the bags of pork rinds, Doritos, and Lay's potato chips. I ran my fingers over some of the bags, listened to the noise they made as I thought about what was inside of them, how we would finally be eating soon. I looked at the candy, and on a separate aisle, the cans of Spam and baked beans lined up in neat little dusty rows.

Then I followed my dad toward the back of the store where the coolers were, not sure of what I would be allowed to purchase. He scanned what was inside them, wiping the condensation from the glass with the palm of his hand, then just stepped back and shook his head. I was waiting for him to say something.

"Just get whatever you want," he finally said. "There's nothing but junk here anyway. I'm going back outside."

"Are you sure?" I asked.

"No, but what other choice do I have? Things can't get much worse for us, can they? You might as well eat garbage too. We can all poison ourselves. It can be just like Jonestown."

"What?" I said. I didn't know what he was talking about.

"Nevermind. Just hurry up. And meet me back in the parking lot when you're done."

"Okay," I said. I wasn't going to argue with him. I was hungry, and I didn't care if the food was bad for us or not.

My dad walked back outside. I heard the little bell over the door sound his exit.

After a few minutes, I had a little red basket full of junk food and was walking up to the counter with it. I knew that both my parents would disapprove of my choices—they always did—but I also knew that they were starving too and would probably eat just about anything at that point.

When I got to the counter I set down a few cans of baked beans, some Spam, a large bag of Lay's potato chips, three glass bottles of Barq's root beer, a loaf of white Bunny bread, some bologna, a pack of sliced cheese, and a gallon of whole milk. While the man was ringing all of this up, the keys of the register clanking like some old typewriter under his oil-stained fingers, I asked him for some fried chicken too. A twelve-piece bucket was only four dollars and I figured I'd have enough money for it.

"Sure thing, bub," he said, adding that to my other purchases. Then he went over to the heated glass case and pulled out a steaming paper bucket full of crispy fried chicken, and he placed it inside of a plastic bag. I thought of the last time my parents and I had tried to eat fried chicken, the disaster that had turned into. I just hoped this would be different.

"That'll be fourteen sixty two," he said, taking the rest of my purchases and putting them into their own bags and then placing them all on top of the counter.

I reached into my back pocket and pulled from it the tract that Darryl had given to me, then opened it and shook out the twenty dollar bill from where it had gotten folded in between its damp pages. The money was crumpled and wet from the rain. But still I passed it across the counter and into the man's open hand.

As he made change, I looked at the tract some more, thinking about how strange it was that this was the second one I had gotten like that. I wondered if I really should tell my parents about it, if this church and its pastor could actually help us.

The register rolled open on its tracks, the change inside the till rattling as the drawer hit the man's jeaned thigh. Then I heard him counting out a pile of dirty coins.

"Five thirty-eight," he said, handing me a five dollar bill, then dropping a bunch of nickels and three dark pennies on top of that.

"Thanks," I said, cramming the money into my pocket, still holding the tract in my hand.

"You go there?" the man asked me, pointing down at the tract.

"Huh?"

"To that church? Is that where you go?"

"No," I said. "I've never been. Some guy handed this to me this morning."

"Well, if you're lookin', bud, that's the place."

I started to pick up the bags with our groceries in them, then dropped the tract into one.

The man watched me. "Don't lose that," he said. "Father will change your life."

"Do you go there?" I asked him.

"I do. Me and my whole family do. And, bud, lemme tell you: it's the best thing that ever happened to us."

"Well, thanks," I said. "Maybe we'll see you there."

"I sure hope so."

I didn't say anything else, just nodded before finally slipping the bags through my hands and walking out of the cool store and back into the late-morning heat. The bell once again clinked overhead and I had to squint my eyes against the glare of sun as I stepped outside. When my eyes finally adjusted, little black spots swam across my vision like tiny fish in an aquarium.

Then I looked across the lot and saw my dad. He was sitting on top of a wooden picnic table, which was beneath a slab of shade cast off by a fat oak tree at the edge of the parking lot. And I noticed for the first time how completely exhausted he looked. But I couldn't blame him. It had been a long morning.

21

When we got back to our truck in the woods, my mother was awake and hanging out clothes to dry on a line she had tied between two pine trees. Nearly everything we owned, it seemed, was soaked from this morning's rain. Even with the tarp covering the back of my dad's pickup truck, water had still gotten in.

My mother's clothes looked damp and her hair was matted down against her shoulders and stuck to her cheeks in dark wet tendrils. I couldn't tell if it was from sweat, humidity, the remnants of the rainstorm, or a combination of all three. She looked terrible and completely miserable standing there like that.

As my dad and I approached, making our way to the little clearing, I could see the steam rising off the hood of the truck and the soggy clothes pulling on the drooping line as my mother hung them up. She had already put our sleeping bags out on the ground to dry but they still looked heavy with moisture and humidity.

"Hi, Rebekah," my dad said as we neared the truck.

My mother didn't say anything.

I could feel her anger crescendoing already, just from our presence, but unlike when we lived on Mr. Tally's property, I would have nowhere to go to escape if my parents started fighting again. I wanted to avert it altogether if I could, so I said, "Here, Mom, we got some food."

I held out the bags.

"Oh, thank God," she said. She stopped what she had been doing and almost ran to where I was standing.

"It's all junk food," my dad interrupted. "Leave it to him to pick out the worst possible things for us to put into our bodies. We'd probably be better off starving," he said.

"Oh, come on, John. Lay off," my mother said. Then she looked at me. "What did you get?"

"Just some chips and stuff," I said. "I got some fried chicken too."

Then she asked, "Where'd you get the money?"

I looked at my dad. He didn't say anything, but I decided that it would be better not to mention the baseball he had tried to use to weigh down the cans, what had happened afterward. I knew then—just as I had known after I had helped my dad slash Mr. Tally's tires—that I would never tell my mother what had happened that morning at the recycling shed. So I lied.

"We just recycled some cans we found on the road this morning," I told her.

"That's great," she said. "How resourceful." It was hard to tell if my mother was being sarcastic or not. But it really didn't matter. I was too hungry to care.

My mother took one of the bags from where it had been hanging on my arm.

"Jeez, Eli," she said. "You really did get a bunch of junk food, didn't you? But you know what? Beggars can't be choosers."

She pulled out the bag of Lay's, tore it open, and then started putting the greasy potato chips into her mouth one after the other.

"There's drinks in here too," I said, putting the plastic bags down on the ground, then digging through them for the root beers. I took one of the glass bottles out and opened it.

My mother glanced over to where my dad was standing in front of the truck. She watched him for a moment as he paced and mumbled, likely disapproving of what we were eating. Then she shook her head and said something under her own breath that I couldn't hear. I was just happy they weren't fighting.

My mother stood next to me for a moment and then she pushed aside her stuff on the open tailgate and sat down.

"Come sit with me," she said, patting the empty space she had created with her hand.

I did. The truck sank down on its shocks in the mud.

My mother picked up the bags and rustled through them some more, pulling everything out and lining it all up on the tailgate. I had forgotten I had tossed the tract into one of them so when she fished that out, I was a little bit nervous as I watched her slowly thumb through it.

"This looks interesting," she said, smiling at me and then looking over her shoulder at my dad to see if he was listening. By then he had already walked away from the truck and into the woods surrounding us and didn't seem to be paying any attention at all to my mother or me anymore. "Where'd you get it?" she asked.

"It was on the counter at the gas station," I lied again. "I thought maybe they could help us."

"Hmmm," she said, still flipping the pages, her greasy fingers smudging the words here and there. She was smiling slightly as she looked through the damp tract.

"So what do you know about this church?" she finally said.

"Nothing. Just what it says there."

She looked at the tract again, continued to thumb through it as if she were thinking about something, not really paying attention to the words on the pages. Inside was all the usual stuff about being born again and accepting Jesus Christ into your life, quotes from Scripture, personal testimonies from people in the community. But my mother kept flipping back to that picture of the man on the front—the one with the long hair and the soft blue eyes.

I wondered if that was the pastor. It wasn't clear but there was something very hypnotic and striking about the image. My mother stared at it like she did with her album covers when she listened to music in her room. I wondered then what had happened to all of her records. Did she still have them? Did she leave them behind? Not much fit in the back of my dad's truck, and since we had to leave so fast that morning when the sheriff had been standing in the yard, watching us, I only imagined that my mother had to leave them. I wondered what Mr. Tally was going to do with all of our stuff that we couldn't take with us.

But it didn't really matter. I had already learned from my parents not to value material, earthly possessions, so what I had owned and left behind was very minimal. Like my dad, I lived an ascetic, monklike sort of existence. I never wanted to get attached to anything. And since we were somewhat nomadic anyway, this seemed to work out in my favor. But I knew my mother really cared about her records, and I felt sorry for her then as she thumbed through that tract, more so than I ever had before. I hoped she would see something in it to give her hope, like that man Darryl had promised it would.

"Maybe we should go here," she finally said, looking up from the pages. "See if they can help us."

"Yeah," I said. "It probably wouldn't hurt."

"Okay. Well, I'll talk to your father about it. Either way, he's going to have to do something. We can't keep living in the woods like this. It's not safe. Not healthy for us as a family. It's just really, really bad. I'm so sorry, Eli. For everything." Her voice started to trail off and I looked over and saw her as she put her face into her hands and started to sob. At first it was just sniffling and low crying, but then her body started to heave and convulse and the noise she made got louder and louder.

I tried to put my hand on her shoulder, something to comfort her, to calm her down. Anything to keep her from going into full hysteria, but my mother just pushed me away. She put her fists in her mouth and screamed, her knuckles white as she bit them and tried to hold back the noise of her pain and frustration over living this life.

She continued to wrack and sob, saying, "I'm sorry, I'm sorry, I'm so so sorry," over and over again, the truck heaving under her, sinking deeper into the mud. The noise of her pain rose above the sounds of the woods: the crickets, the tree branches dripping rainwater onto the ground, the woodpeckers high overhead and tapping away at the soggy bark.

I watched as the tract finally slid from my mother's leg and fell onto the ground at her feet, which dangled slightly from the open tailgate. I bent down and picked it up, put it in my back pocket and then just walked off into the woods, away from her crying, away from my dad's stoic wandering on the other side of the clearing, where he was surely pretending not to hear my mother as he whittled away at a branch with his thumbnail.

There was nothing I could do about anything.

I just walked far enough so that I could no longer hear or see my parents. I sat down on the wet ground, feeling the dampness immediately soak through my jeans, wetting my legs. listened to the woods around me, feeling helpless and alone. I was tired and hungry.

And then I put my face in my dirty hands and started to cry. Just like my mother was doing in the back of our truck. I looked down and let my tears fall onto the muddy duff of pine and brown grass surrounding my soggy, pathetic shoes.

22

I don't know how long I sat there crying like that, but I was surprised when I heard my dad calling my name some time later. I hadn't heard my parents fighting, and I certainly wasn't far enough away from them to not have noticed it. I wasn't sure what was going on.

As I stood up, my pants were still wet and stuck to my legs, my feet sinking into the mud as I walked back to the clearing where our truck was parked and from where my dad's voice was calling. I could hear the water sucking at my shoes as if the ground were trying to swallow me. I wished it would.

When I finally came through the wall of pines and thick deadfall that made up the perimeter of the clearing, I saw a small trash fire just beside my dad's truck, into whose hungry flames my mother was tossing a pile of soggy books, the ropes of smoke rising up like dark gray tendrils into the web of branches overhead.

The sun had moved westward during the time I was off in the woods crying—maybe I had fallen asleep after all, I don't remember—and with the shade cast down from the canopy of trees, it felt as though we were in what my dad sometimes called the gloaming hour. I still wasn't sure what time it was though.

My mother's face showed no emotion—which was actually more frightening than if she had been completely hysterical—as she tossed those books into the hungry fire. The pages were still heavy with rainwater and barely fluttered as she threw them in.

The damp books threatened to extinguish the flames with their own moisture, but occasionally my mother would squirt a stream of lighter fluid onto it all, feeding the fire so that it would consume everything she fed it.

While she did this, my dad was leaning against the hood of his truck and rocking it back and forth, trying to free it from the hole it was in. Between the rain from the night before and our sleeping and sitting in it, the truck had sunk almost up to the middle of the tires in thick black mud.

When my dad looked up and saw me, he said, "Eli, come over here. I need you to help me with this."

I nodded at him, then walked past my mother, trying not to make eye contact with her as she stoically fed the fire, squeezing the little yellow bottle of Ronson lighter fluid that my dad had used to fill his Zippo with, a clear arc of it misting the flames until they grew and grew and grew, turning everything into dark ash. I could see the angry orange tendrils reflected in my mother's damp eyes.

If I had ever been frightened of my mother's behavior in the past (and I had been, many times), never had it affected me as deeply as it did then—seeing her wild eyes glimmering in the flame light. My mother seemed to look right through me. It was as though I weren't even there. She reminded me of one of those shell-shocked soldiers from an old World War II photograph I had seen once, flipping through the moldy pages of an outdated encyclopedia set we had lying around. A book that may have very well been burning in the fire right then. Then I looked away and into the direction where my dad stood, uselessly rocking the truck in the mud.

He stopped and went around to the driver's side door as I approached.

"I want you to push from behind," he said. "Get it to rock back and forth like I was doing. I'm going to get in and try to give it some gas and hopefully drive it out of this hole. We got ourselves into a real mess here this time, Eli."

My dad could have been speaking literally or figuratively then, it didn't matter. I just did what he said, trying to ignore the fire my mother was feeding behind us, the terrible sound of all that paper burning and dying.

I walked over to the back of the truck. I was careful not to get too close to the heat of the flames, my mother listlessly tossing books and even some clothes into them, occasionally squirting streams of lighter fluid to keep them going.

Then I pushed aside the plastic bags on the open tailgate where my mother had left them, realizing that despite how hungry I had been, I still hadn't even eaten any of the food that I had gotten. The fried chicken looked cold already in its greasy bucket, a couple of small white feathers, browned by grease, poking up from the fried skin. The bottles of root beer looked warm now and were probably flat too from the truck's perpetual rocking. I looked at it all sitting there, how sad and pathetic everything was, and then I just gentled the tailgate shut so I could get a good hold on it and help my dad push us out of the mud.

My dad had already started the engine and a little cloud of smoke was chuffing up from the rusted-out exhaust pipe and into my face. It burnt my eyes and the back of my throat so I covered my mouth and nose with my hand until the exhaust diminished, then I leaned against the back of the truck and started heaving at it with my weight, careful not to slip in the mud under my feet. Once I had it rocking back and forth pretty good, my dad gave it a little gas. The tires spun but did nothing but spray more wet mud onto my jeans.

I pushed again and saw the tires edge the tip of the rut and then my dad gave it a little more gas and the truck rolled out of the hole and onto the flat ground just beyond it. He drove up a few feet and then he shut off the engine and climbed out of the cab.

"Good job," he said. "Now we can finally get out of here soon."

"Where are we gonna go?" I said.

"Well, your mother and I talked about it. We're going to go to that church. See if someone there can help us."

I looked at my mother, who had stopped tossing our stuff into the fire. Now she was just standing there, looking out into the woods at something that I couldn't see.

"We still need to get rid of a lot of stuff," my dad was saying. "They won't take us in if we have too many things to worry them with. So I need you to help your mother burn anything we don't absolutely need for survival."

"What if they don't help us?" I said. "Then what are we going to do?"

"I don't know, but either way we need to clean house, Eli. All of these material possessions that we have are weighing us down. Don't you see that they literally got us stuck in that hole over there? God's trying to tell us something, without a doubt."

I didn't answer him. We had lost almost everything we owned already when Mr. Tally kicked us off his property. Now this. I looked toward the truck and our meager possessions that were in its bed, wondered what getting rid of those things could possibly do to help our situation, but knew it wouldn't do any good to try to talk him out of it.

My mother had already given up, it seemed, and so I didn't try to protest either. Instead, I just walked over to the truck, opened the tailgate, and started dragging stuff out, letting it fall into the mud wherever it wanted to fall. I didn't care. I even took out and tossed my "Just Say No" comic strip, which the school board had sent back to us after the fair was over and that somehow seemed responsible for setting everything that was happening at that moment into motion, all of our bad luck. I would be glad to see it burn.

My dad was unclipping our clothes from the line that my mother had set up for them to dry on, and for every one thing he folded and piled next to his feet, he threw three things off into the woods. Some of our shirts and pants and socks got caught in the tiny branches and the deadfall and so the woods around us started to look like the aftermath of a tornado. I looked behind me to see where my mother was.

At first I couldn't see her. The fire had died down and the smoke coming up from the charred books, clothes, and blackened branches was thick, creating a sort of curtain between me and where my mother had been standing. But then I saw her. She was sitting against the bole of a wispy pine tree, her knees tucked up under her chin, her gaunt arms wrapped around her shins. She was rocking back and forth, her movements not much different from how my dad's truck had rocked when we heaved it out of the mud just minutes before. She looked mechanical, stoic, detached. I had never seen my mother look or act this bad.

She seemed gone. Her eyes were open, but I could tell she wasn't looking at anything. Just that same faraway stare as when she had thrown those books, one by one, into the fire. I wanted to hug her, but was afraid she'd scream at me, or worse, hit me—smack me for startling her out of her own mental retreat from life.

Then my dad was walking toward me with a small pile of folded shirts and pants, our three sleeping bags, and the ripped plastic tarp in his arms. It was all we had left to put back in the truck.

I lift a pack of cigarettes off the dashboard and shake one out, push in the lighter—a little black button with a picture of a cigarette and a wavy white line of smoke coming out of the tip—next to the radio. The console is melted a little bit around where the lighter goes, my dad trying too many times in the dark to put the glowing-hot button back in its place after lighting one of his cigars—a habit he had started and stopped innumerable times over the years.

After it clicks out, I hold the orange coils up to the end of my cigarette and light it, blowing out a thick gray cloud of smoke through the half-open window.

I drive down the deserted streets of Franklinton, a few caution lights swaying in the breeze on their black overhead lines, a single yellow light blinking incessantly, a soft glow against the night-glistened asphalt. Like a heartbeat in a sleeping body, whose rhythm is projected onto a computer monitor—all those lines like the peaks and valleys of a mountain range.

I keep going, right through town and south toward the highway, eventually crossing the Chess Richardson Memorial Bridge, the river passing underneath it black under the moonglow, the shoals a bright white, the color of bleached bones.

Then I'm on Highway 25 heading south.

The only light in the cab is from the radio and the glowing orange tics and numbers on the dashboard. Outside, though, it is almost completely dark. And it feels as if I am hemmed in on both sides by trees, tall skinny pines that line the hilled road from Franklinton all the way to Folsom, then seem to give way to the squat buildings and gas stations as you pass through town, only to appear again and stay there for a while more—like a fence reaching up into the sky all the way until you get to Covington, which is where I'm headed.

There's really nothing out here but woods, the occasional trailer set off and away from the road in a small clearing in the brush, a sorry trashfire smoldering in the yard, a couple of dogs chained to the bole of some wispy tree. But at night, and on the road, you can't even really see that stuff anyway.

Everything out here—including the people—is practically drowning in darkness, the black asphalt of the highway, the yellow road markers ticking off one after the other before becoming a single line at the foot of one of the many hills between here and Folsom—the myriad reflectors catching your headlights and keeping you on your side of the road, telling you where to go. Where you belong.

The highway spools out underneath the truck's tires—the same truck my dad had used to take me to the fair where I had won that knife. The same truck we slept in after Mr. Tally kicked us out of our house, and probably the only reason why I'm here right now.

The occasional logging truck roars past me on the other side of the road, its mass shaking the little pickup I'm driving as if it were a toy. Sometimes I can hear the pieces of wood hitting the windshield when those trucks pass, chips of bark flying from the chained stacks of trees, which look like a pile of matches belonging to some fairytale giant who lives somewhere out in these woods and comes out at night to scare children.

The logs have little orange flags nailed to the ends of them where they hang out past the boundaries of the tractor-trailer, bent downward and nearly scraping at the surface of the road. I've heard lots of stories of cars following too closely behind these trucks and running right into the back of them. And I can imagine one of those logs going right through my own windshield, obliterating me and everything else in the cab. Is it wrong for me to wish for that sometimes? To wish I could start my life over? Try again?

As I pass through Folsom, driving under the yellow wash of its one blinking caution light (just like the one in Franklinton), then past the only police cruiser in town—the officer inside probably dozing off at this hour, his rolls of mottled flesh drooping over his uniform's collar like candlewax, melting under the soft blue-green glow of his cruiser's console—I look over to my right and see the old Sunflower grocery store looming in the distance. The store's dark inside, its large windows covered with signs that advertise all the things they have for sale: Milk, Bread, Ice. Cigarettes.

I look at the cracked dashboard of my dad's pickup truck, press down on my own pack of cigarettes, which is almost empty now, then look at the gas gauge, whose needle is hovering just above the E. Then I make a decision. Or maybe all of this had already been decided for me a very long time ago—the pull of fate like a tide going out to sea. But who can ever really know these things?

I turn off the highway, click my headlights so no one will see me, then pull into the gravel-and-asphalt lot behind the store. After I turn off the truck, I reach over to the glove compartment and flick it open, take out the flashlight that my dad keeps buried in there under stacks of maps and other yellowed papers.

Then I climb out of the cab, gentling the door shut and stuffing the keys in my pocket, feeling a tinge of guilt as I look at the key ring my dad keeps on them, which is a little white circle with the words "JESUS LOVES YOU" written in bold red letters. I don't think he even believes that anymore. For him, it's probably just something to keep on your keys so they're easier to find.

I look in the bed of the truck, the same corrugated surface on which I had spent a lot of long nights over the years, my mother and father cocooned beside me in their dirty sleeping bags, all of us trying to sleep and not think about the days preceding us and the even longer ones that were likely to come.

Then I root around through the rusty tools that my dad keeps stacked in red plastic milk crates—pulling out long screwdrivers, wrenches, a hammer—until I find what I'm looking for: a crowbar. I pick it up and thread it through the belt loop of my Rustler jeans.

The gravel crunches under my feet as I trundle across the parking lot.

I creep behind the store—the beam from my flashlight limning the graffiti spray-painted on an old dumpster back there. I can make out some names and dates, a couple of crudely drawn pentagrams with the numbers 666 sprayed beneath them. It all seems to glow under the flashlight's white coruscating beam.

I keep waiting for someone to rise up from the flattened piles of cardboard boxes and plastic crates, a torn coat or stained blanket enshrouding their gaunt and dirty frame, sheaths of soggy newspaper fluttering down from them as they slowly stand to see who's intruding their space—their bloodshot eyes bright against their dirt-smeared face, the reek of cheap whiskey emanating from a toothless maw as they croak at me in a hardly-used voice, "Who's there?"

I just try to ignore all of this as I pry open the door and creep inside.

1

The Light of His Way Baptist Church was a small building that you could see from Highway 62 as you came into town. It was nestled in a clearing that was carved out among a sea of loblolly pines and a few scattered pin oaks, all trying to reach their way up through the trash trees and toward the sun.

To get there, you passed thick woods pocked with sandpits full of clear, almost blue water and drove over miles and miles of gray asphalt veined with tar that had been used to fill the endless, heat-fueled cracks in the road. Most of the land had POSTED signs nailed to the trees, and across the steep ditch was a stretch of what seemed to be endless lengths of steel fence or barbed wire.

The church building itself looked more like one of those old-time schoolhouses except that it was painted white—and instead of a bell on top, there was a skinny wooden cross that seemed to stab at the sky around it. There was a sign in front of the building, just to the side of the gravel road that led up to it, with the name of the church, "The Light of His Way," hand-painted with dark blue smears of paint. Beneath that were the words "Come As You Are."

This place was different from some of the other churches we'd attended over the years. I can remember the strip-mall sanctuaries, the little churches in a leased-out space right next to a Family Dollar or a Goodwill. There was always a coldness to those places that I couldn't quite understand—something sterile almost. We had also gone to church at people's houses sometimes—before my parents moved us onto Mr. Tally's land—or little wooden barns in their backyards or in the middle of some horse field. We listened to sermons sitting in the grass while the preacher stood on his front porch and yelled down at us, spit flying out of his mouth in wide, angry arcs.

It seemed as though we went to a different church every week back then, before things started to get really bad and we ended up alone on Mr. Tally's farm, then homeless. But as soon as we stepped inside The Light of His Way, my parents smiled at me and both of them held my hand as we walked down the aisle toward the pulpit and sat in the hard wooden pews. Something had come over them, it seemed, and I think it was being inside of this building that had done it.

As the man we would later learn to call "Father" slowly approached the dais, he came up the aisle and shook hands with the men of the congregation, bent down to hug some of the women and their children. This was indeed the same man pictured on the front of the tract I had been given: his long, brown hair dusting his shoulders, his thick beard.

When he got to the front of the sanctuary and noticed us—his new congregants—he reached out and shook my dad's hand. "Welcome," he said. Then he looked over at my mother and smiled at her and took her hand too. "We're happy to have you join us today," he said.

My mother smiled at him and then the preacher looked at me and extended his hand. I took it with my small fingers and noticed right away how soft his skin was, as though he had never spent a day of his life outdoors. But there was a warmth there I couldn't explain: it was nothing like I had ever felt in a church before. Maybe it was because we were all so desperate then, but still it was comforting.

"Welcome, young man," he said to me before continuing up to the dais. "I'm happy to have you in the Lord's house."

The preacher was dressed in jeans and work boots, a red-and-black checkered flannel shirt tucked into his pants to reveal a thick brown leather belt with a square buckle made of scrimshawed pewter inlaid with turquoise and leather coils. His hair was combed back, his thick beard almost eclipsing his ears and hiding half of his tanned, sandpaper cheeks. I couldn't keep my eyes off him. When he finally reached the pulpit, he placed his cracked leather Bible on the rough surface of the dais and then he opened it so that the rostrum was nearly covered by the book.

Then he just stood there, surveying his congregants and smiling down at us.

I looked around too. I noticed a couple of familiar faces from town, though there was no one I knew by name. I thought I saw that man Darryl from the recycling yard—the one who had given me the tract—but he looked different, with a white shirt buttoned all the way up to his neck and tucked into his jeans. I wasn't even sure if that was really him or not.

When I turned back around to face the preacher again, I noticed someone else I had met before too: she was sitting in the front row, dressed in a similar pantsuit like the one she had been wearing at the fair. It was the woman who had commented on my comic strip. The first person who had given me a tract about this place. The same pillbox purse was sitting next to her on the softly pillowed pew.

She didn't seem to notice me though. She was so focused on watching the dais and the man standing behind it.

"Good morning," he finally said, smiling, his voice carrying across the sanctuary like a strong gust of air.

"Good morning, Father," the congregation said back, a field of welcoming voices singing in unison.

I looked over at my parents and both of them were staring up at Father, transfixed. Like everyone else, they seemed enraptured by him.

"Let us thank the Lord for the gift of this day," he continued. "Let us all rejoice and thank Him for the promise of our Salvation, for everlasting life. Amen."

The congregants did this, softly speaking "thank yous" and "Amens" and "hallelujahs" in their own private way. I looked around the small sanctuary. Everyone inside seemed to be smiling, the warm sun coming in through the tall windows on either side of us, an audible hum pulsing in the air, as though electricity were flowing through the building.

After that, everyone sat calmly, the women with their hands in their laps, the sea of their long, denim dresses blooming around their fingers. Some of them held onto their husband's arms, gently, as if waiting for someone to tell them something. Which, in a way, I guess, they were. Because it was then that Father began to speak again.

"I want to read to you today from Matthew, Chapter Eight, Verse Twenty-three," Father said. He opened his Bible and slowly turned the pages, which looked thin as onionskin; you could hear them crackling under his thick fingers. You could see through them almost—the black printed letters against the off-white paper—as the sun came down in a thick cylinder and landed on the podium.

Some of the congregants flipped through the pages in their own Bibles, which they had picked up from a wooden slot in the pew in front of them, trying to find where Father was about to read from. My parents did this too, while some of the others just sat there, looking up at the man at the dais, their eyes almost misty with adoration.

"And here," Father said, "it says that when Jesus got into the boat, His disciples followed him. But suddenly a violent storm came upon the sea. Their boat was engulfed by waves and water, but Jesus was sleeping. Sleeping!" Father pounded his hand onto the podium, a little chuff of dusty air coming up from around his Bible. He looked around at us in order to let this image of Christ asleep on the endangered boat really sink in.

Then he continued talking in his low, lilting voice. "My friends, Jesus's disciples went and woke Him now, saying, 'Lord, save us! We are perishing!' but Jesus replied to them, saying, 'You of little faith. Why are you so afraid?' Then he stood and rebuked the winds and the sea and the waves, and all was perfectly calm. His disciples were amazed then, asking 'What kind of man is this? Even the wind and the sea obey Him!'"

Father looked up again, seemingly waiting for everyone to notice him. "Even the wind and the sea obey Him," he repeated.

"Amen," said the congregants, my parents' voices becoming part of the call and response now. I joined them as well.

"Brothers and sisters," Father said. "I want to tell you a story. I think you'll find it fitting with that bit of scripture you just heard. Listen . . . .

"When I was a boy, probably about nine or ten, my father took me out on his shrimp boat. I remember we left our house in the middle of the night to drive down to Grand Isle so we could get out on the water before the sun came up. There was no sign of bad weather that morning, but it was cold. I remember that—it was the dead of winter, or at least that's what it felt like. The gulf was a little rough when we set off, a few breakers and white-caps at the shore-line, but once we got out there and the sun started coming up, the water was smooth as glass.

"My father put the trawl lines down and I sat next to him as he drank his coffee and we trawled the water. Everything was quiet. But out of nowhere, it seemed, a squall line started to pass near us. It was like a thick, gray wall of clouds overhead, low and omi-nous. Have you ever seen a storm come in over the water before, my brothers and sisters? Well, that's what this was. And it was ugly."

The people in the pews just nodded, as though they had all experienced this.

Father continued: "I remember the boat started to heave back and forth. My father put his Thermos down and went to the wheel to try to steer us away from the storm. Then the boat rocked hard to the right and his Thermos fell over—I remember the sound it made when it hit the boat—how it spilled hot black coffee into the hull. It was like a bunch of tiny dark rivers—or veins—on the ridged metal beneath our feet. To this day, that image still stands out in my mind. It's amazing the seeds the Lord plants in us, isn't it? The memories they create?"

The way Father spoke was like listening to someone read a poem, only he wasn't reading any of this. His eyes were mostly closed as he spoke; otherwise, he was looking out at us, everyone's mouths half-open in awe and wonder.

"The storm was on us now," he went on. "Our boat was like a piece of driftwood being tossed around in a whirlpool. And it had all happened that fast." Father snapped his fingers above his head in order to emphasize the quickness of the storm's arrival. Then he said, "The water was swelling beneath us and we would go up in our little boat, then the bow would seem to point almost straight down as we descended along the face of the swell, barreling toward that floor of dark water below.

"Rain was pelting my face. It stung my flesh. I was crying, begging my father to do something. He was holding that wheel, my brothers and sisters, and I could see the skin where it was pulled taut against his knuckles. He wrestled with that wheel, keeping the boat on course as best he could.

"But you know what was amazing? When I saw my father's face as he turned back to check on me, he was smiling. He didn't really look happy, but he looked at peace with himself, at peace with what was happening to us, at peace with what might happen—all of the dark possibilities of death, of drowning.

"Then a heavy spray of water splashed over the side of the boat and blocked him from my view, wetting my clothes and hair. I slid off my seat and fell down, then covered my head with my hands, just waiting for the boat to flip over. I was already holding my breath, expecting to go into that angry water at any moment.

"But we never did.

"My father kept the boat steady until we were just beyond that dark, gray scud of clouds, and we headed back toward the shoreline. When the storm was behind us, I asked him if he had been scared, and he told me that he was, but he knew that whatever happened, all would be fine. That's what he said. Nothing else. He never talked about any of it again, never told my mother. Nobody. Such was the depth of his faith, his trust in the workings of the Lord."

Father paused and looked around to let what he had just told us sink in. Then he continued, moving now from behind the pulpit and walking across the raised platform at the front of the church, leaving his Bible folded open on the rostrum.

"Do you know that when I first saw this scripture I just read to you," he said, "I knew it was exactly like what my father and I had been through? It was as though Jesus had been on that boat with us that day. Calming the waters, seeing us through the storm. And we know that His eternal promise is that, if you believe in Him, He will stay with you through any hurricane or earthquake or storm that this tiny world can muster!"

"Amen!" Now everyone was suddenly standing again, some of the men with their Bibles held above their heads in one hand, the spine folded over their fingers, the pages flapping like wings. People were clapping and smiling and crying. I had never seen anything quite like it before. Most of the churches we had been to previously were somber, quiet events, with low music and restrained discussions. Or, otherwise, the pastor was just angry.

But this was alive. My parents were standing now too, waving their arms above their heads. I watched at first, cautiously, but then stood myself once I realized I was the only person still sitting.

"And do you know?" Father was shouting now over the noise. "Do you know, my brothers and sisters in Christ, that sometimes the Lord appoints one man to stand in His place until the day comes that He returns to rapture our souls to Heaven?"

"Yes!"

"And do you know that on that day, it wasn't my father, as I had originally thought, nor was it the hand of God that calmed those waters? That it was me who got us through that storm?"

"Yes!"

"That I was just like Jesus on that boat with his disciples? I was lying there, as though I were asleep, and I calmed that angry water."

"You did, Father! You calmed it!"

"It took me years to accept that, brothers and sisters, but I know now that it's true. That I am here to calm the storms of your lives—if you give yourself over to me. Like it says in the book of Matthew, 'Come to me, all of you who are weary and burdened, and I will give you rest!'"

"Amen!" everyone shouted—even my parents' voices echoed throughout the church.

People were crying now, hugging each other and falling into their pews, knees too weak to hold them up any longer. It was a spectacle like I had never seen before.

I looked over at my parents. They seemed just as rapt as everyone else. They were holding hands and my mother was weeping quiet tears, sobbing, her chest heaving with the effort. My dad put his arm around me and clasped my shoulder with his thick hand.

I closed my eyes and listened to the sounds of the church, felt the warmth of the sun on my cheeks. I tried to be overcome. I wanted to believe this was the change we needed in our lives. But something in me wouldn't allow for that yet.

Now Father was turning to pick up an acoustic guitar from where it rested in its metal stand next to the dais. He pulled the canvas strap across his chest, then adjusted a metal capo over the third fret, finally strumming a D chord before easing into "Amazing Grace." Everyone else just sang along with him.

2

By the time the song was over, it had started to rain outside. You could hear it hitting the roof and the thunder booming overhead. Father put down his guitar and disappeared from the stage, leaving the inside of the church quiet and still.

My mother grabbed my hand and held it as the room slowly got darker, almost completely black. Then a single cylinder of white-blue light shone down onto the dais where Father had been preaching and singing. I looked back and then up toward the gallery behind the pews and saw what looked like a large black cannon, the light emanating from its long tube, but I couldn't see who was controlling it. My mother nudged at me to look ahead, to pay attention.

That's when Father came back out from someplace at the front of the church. I hadn't seen or heard a door opening—not when he left the stage and not now as he was returning to it. It was almost as though he had materialized out of the air. The next moment he was standing at the dais under the bright light and looking out at us as the thunder and rain beat down outside the church.

"Brothers and sisters, for the second half of the service, we have something very special planned for you," Father said. "I know it's not easy staying here on this rainy morning like this, but I promise to make it worth your trouble."

Father held both sides of the podium as the rain outside glazed the windows behind him and then a streak of lightning bloomed in the dark, gray clouds, making the sanctuary laden with light, heavy with it. Several of the women jumped and gasped out loud.

Father just smiled at all of this.

"It's okay," he said. "Our Lord has us under His wing. We're all safe in here."

Then, as if in response, thunder rumbled again from outside in the distance. Father seemed to ignore it this time. He said, "My brothers and sisters, could you please stand and help me welcome a special guest?"

As the congregants rose and the overhead lights came back on, I heard the large doors at the back of the sanctuary open on their giant hinges. Two women in ankle-length dresses were now walking through the opening, both of them flanking a man slouched over in a wheelchair.

The man was wearing a green Army jacket, he had a long beard and hair that cascaded in greasy iron-gray strands from his stained Mack Truck hat, and his eyes had a far-off look, lidded and puffy as though he were half-asleep. We all looked as this man was wheeled down the aisle toward the front of the church. Father had come around from behind the podium then and was waiting there on the raised platform, his arms spread forth like an eagle's wings.

The rain pounded the roof. We all stood still. Watching.

When the man in the wheelchair was parked in front of the congregation, Father bent down toward him and whispered something into his ear. The man looked up suddenly, like he had been awakened from a long nap. Then he looked out at the congregants as though he hadn't seen any of us before that moment.

Father stood and now his voice boomed forth over the rain and the thunder outside. "Brothers and sisters, this is Leon," he said.

"Leon has joined us this morning with a tremendous effort. You see, brothers and sisters, Leon is paralyzed. He feels nothing from the middle of his chest all the way down to his toes. Nothing at all."

I looked around and it seemed as though everyone was completely entranced, some of the women standing slack-jawed while their husbands stood beside them with their fists clenched at their sides.

"Leon is a veteran," Father continued. "He served our great country overseas in Vietnam and paid for our freedom with his mobility—the very thing that makes us human, which so many of us take for granted. Can I get an Amen?"

It took almost a second or two for everyone to snap back out from their stupor, but then we all said it: "Amen!"

"Louder!"

"A-men!"

"I think Leon deserves to walk again, my brothers and sisters, don't you?"

"Yes, Father!"

"Jesus wants Leon to walk again. Jesus wants Leon to be able to play football with his son, to walk out to the bus stop in the after-noons and meet his children when they get home from school!"

"Hallelujah!"

Within that short amount of time, the electricity, as before, seemed to have increased in the room so that you could almost feel it in the air. Much like you could sense it outside as those myriad veins of lightning trailed out and across the heavy, gray skies.

"Jesus has asked me to heal this man. And with His help, broth-ers and sisters, I intend to do that very thing."

"Amen!"

"Before you," Father said, "is a healer. A fixer." He wiped his fore-head with the sleeve of his flannel shirt. "Do you believe in me?"

"Yes, Father! We believe in you!"

Leon still sat somewhat slouched over in his chair as before but I could see his chest heaving outward then falling, his shoulders going back and forth as he breathed deeper and deeper in anticipa-tion of what was going to happen to him.

"Brothers and sisters, pray with me," Father said. He put his head down and we all closed our eyes in silent prayer. I didn't know what to say so I just thought about what it would be like if I were unable to move my legs. I touched my thighs with my fingers and tried to imagine if they couldn't send the signal back up to my brain to make them move. It made them ache just thinking about it.

Then I heard the click of a microphone coming on and the brief, high-pitched whine of feedback as one of the women who had helped Leon to the front of the church brought a black mike down from behind the podium and handed it to Father. When he spoke into it, his voice seemed to wash down from the rafters in warm pulsing waves.

"Leon," Father started, moving the mike in front of the man's face, "could you tell these folks just a little bit about yourself before we begin?"

Father was holding the mike just under Leon's jaw, waiting for him to say something. Then Leon cleared his throat and another brief whine of feedback came out of the overhead speakers. Father pulled back the mike a couple of inches.

"Well, my name's Leon, like you done said already," the man began. He looked weak, nervous. "I live out by way of Sun with my wife and two boys. When I was in the war over in 'Nam, I took some shrapnel in the back and lost all feelin' in both my legs. Haven't walked in twenty years."

I was thinking about the math of this and couldn't understand how Leon could have two school-aged children if he had served in Vietnam, had lost all feeling from the chest down twenty years ago. I tried to push the thought back as Father leaned the mike closer to his own face now.

"Well, how would you like to walk again today, Leon?"

"Bud, if you could make me walk again, I'd kiss your feet in front of all these people." The congregation laughed nervously at the interruption of the otherwise somber moment. Leon looked skeptical, but he seemed more alert now than he did when they first wheeled him in.

"There won't be any need for that, brother, but the Lord has touched my shoulder and I promise you, in His name, that you will walk out of this building today. On your own two feet! We can roll that chair of yours out into the rain for the pigeons to roost on!"

"Hallelujah!" someone in the crowd shouted. Then the rest of the congregants began to clap. A manic energy was starting to build up in the room again. The clapping started to take on a rhythmic beat as Father set the mike down onto the stage and lifted the crippled man from his chair. His legs were completely limp and looked like two waterlogged branches as Father held him upright from the crooks underneath his arms.

Then he pushed the wheelchair back and set Leon down onto the carpeted floor so that we could all see him. He looked like a doctor about to operate on a patient. Father was speaking to him, but I couldn't hear what he was saying with the clapping going on and the rain outside.

By then some of the congregants started to move into the aisle at the center of the sanctuary in order to get a better look at what was happening up front. I just stood on the tips of my toes and peered over the people in front of me as best I could. Then I watched as Father placed his hands flat against Leon's chest. You could see his fingers going up and down with each heavy breath that Leon took.

Then Father closed his eyes and started to speak in tongues, slowly sliding his hands down to Leon's limp legs, holding his fingers there for a moment before both men started to heave and convulse as though electricity were passing between their bodies.

Outside lightning struck again. The lights in the church flickered off and several women screamed. It was almost completely dark now. Father didn't stop, though. He continued to hold his hands on the man's legs and he continued speaking in tongues, the sounds emanating from his mouth getting louder and louder, completely incoherent now. Some of the people in the church looked on wide-eyed and in terror. A couple of them had moved up front so that they were standing directly over Father, but they seemed afraid to touch him.

Then we saw it. The man's legs started to move, kicking up and down as Father's hands remained covering them. Leon started to moan as though he were in pain. A couple of the people standing over Father stepped away from him now. Inside the church was still dark, the only light a sporadic orange glow from the soft lighting at either side of the aisle and a couple of emergency lights in the wooden rafters overhead.

Another pop of lightning outside and then everything seemed to stop. My mother put her arm around my shoulder and pulled me toward her. My dad was standing still. Only his shoulders seemed to rise and fall, subtly as he took in and exhaled breath. I could no longer see what was happening at the front of the church, but I suddenly heard a collective gasp from some of the people in the pews closest to where Father was and then, in the dim orange glow from the aisle lights, I saw him stand up, his hands clasped in prayer before he raised them over his head in jubilation.

He was no longer speaking in tongues, but was whispering softly to himself—words I couldn't make out from where I was standing—and then he looked up toward the rafters and all of the church lights suddenly came back on. Father's eyes were closed but I could see the light overhead reflecting off of two straight streams of tears that leaked from his eyelids and then rolled down into his glistening beard before disappearing somewhere behind his ears. Father was crying. But he never looked down at Leon, who was now slowly standing up on legs that just moments ago had appeared useless, limp, dead.

The congregants erupted into applause. My mother took her arm from around my shoulder and lifted her hands above her head and clapped too. My dad did the same. I followed their lead, but I was still unsure about what I had just witnessed.

"Praise the Lord! Hallelujah! Amen!" the crowd was shouting now, still clapping furiously, as if overtaken by the same electrical energy Father had just channeled out of himself and into this man who was now standing, moving back and forth at the front of the church on his new legs. Had Father really healed him? Was this really happening? After all the things my parents had taught me, after the great distrust and doubt and cynicism they had planted in me over the years, here they both were taking part in this, letting themselves be overwhelmed with passion for a man we didn't even know. A man who had just done something that was very hard to believe.

Leon shook Father's hand—they were both crying now—and then Leon started to run around the pews, all the way to the back of the sanctuary, people clapping him on the back as he passed them. There were more tears, shouts of joy, jubilation.

Father had to pick up the mike again to make his voice heard over the commotion. "Brothers and sisters!" he shouted. "You have just witnessed a miracle! The Lord has entered our sanctuary, our little country church, and has proven His power over us! We are in His house! Let us rejoice!"

"Amen!" we all shouted.

By now, Leon was making his way to the front of the church again, where he dramatically picked up his old wheelchair and held it over his head like a barbell. He ran back down the aisle with it and charged through the open doors and into the foyer, where we heard the outermost doors open onto the rain. Then we could hear the metal chair clanking in the gravel and against the sidewalk as he tossed it outside. More applause and shouting. Laughter too.

Leon came back in on his two strong legs and walked up to the front of the church and stood next to Father, who started to speak again.

"Leon," he said. "How do you feel, brother?"

"Bud, I haven't felt this good since I was twenty years old! Thank you, Father! Amen and Hallelujah!"

"No, Leon. Please don't thank me. Let us all thank the Lord for His Glory."

Father's voice was measured now, calm. He looked tired. He put his head down in prayer and he held Leon's hand as he spoke. There were tears among the congregants in the pews and I could hear people sniffling and whispering to one another about what had just happened.

They were saying we had witnessed a miracle.

3

We started attending The Light of His Way every Sunday after that. Father had taken us in and had given us a place to sleep, food to eat. We quickly became involved with the church's extracurricular activities as well: Wednesday prayer groups, the potluck dinners on Friday nights.

As part of our service, and as a sort of payment for our room and board, my mother and father and I were all assigned to help clear land behind the church. It was hard work but it was important, Father told us, so that we could eventually use the entire spread to live on, raise cows, pigs, chickens. We'd plant a series of large vegetable gardens too, he said—even build housing out of a fleet of old school buses he had found and would soon be purchasing for us. It would become a self-sustaining community where we could all live in peace and love and in harmony. We would call it The Lord's Acre.

On Wednesdays, we had Bible study. The entire congregation would gather outside of the church, sit in the freshly mown grass, and Father would read to us from Scripture, some passage he liked, and then he would sermonize on it for however long the spirit moved him to do so. It was never less than an hour—sometimes going nonstop for even two or three—but no one seemed to mind. Mothers held their children in their laps, fathers sat next to their families on large quilts or picnic blankets, and everyone just listened. We were all held rapt by this man who had taken us into his fold.

Father's sermons were different from anything I'd ever heard before. He talked about his life, his childhood, his long-suffering mother and then the people who took care of him after she suddenly died when he was ten. He had never really known his father, he told us, had only seen him sporadically throughout his life— which made the parable he told during that first sermon my parents and I heard seem as strange as that man Leon having school-aged children. But I was learning to ignore these inconsistencies, as my parents seemed to accept everything Father told us without question.

He told us about how, after his mother died, he was moved from one foster home to another, how he never knew where he would be from one week to the next. He started to run away when he was just thirteen years old, he said, only to end up in a juvenile detention center for trying to steal a car.

Father told us about how he worked in the fields there, said that's where he had learned about and had come to love agriculture. He told us that he also became aware of the hierarchies that formed in places like that, how you had to either be strong—or at least have the appearance of being strong—in order to survive in detention.

There were many fights, he told us, between him and the other boys. Sometimes he came out on top, he said, and sometimes he didn't. But he always walked away feeling stronger than he was before, as though he had learned something. He said we should always remember how David had defeated Goliath with just that one stone. Our enemies were never as big as they appeared, he told us, and with the Lord at our backs, there was no one we couldn't defeat.

Once Father told us something he said he had never mentioned to anyone else before. It was important to him, he said, that we as his congregation knew all there was to know of him, that if we were to follow him—truly follow him, body and soul—that we must know exactly who we were following, and why. He stood there at his rostrum that day, wiping his face with the sleeve of his flannel shirt. Even in the summer, Father always wore a long-sleeved flannel shirt and jeans with muddy brown work boots.

We watched in silence as he gripped the edges of the dais, prepared himself as we waited for him to speak.

"My brothers and sisters," he said. "What I'm about to tell you will shock you. It may make you see me in a different light. It may even make some of you want to leave. But the Lord has spoken to me—has spoken to my heart—and He told me that I must share with you my greatest sin if I am to continue to lead you in His name."

There was a palpable shift in the congregants then, as though everyone sat forward in their seats a bit. I placed my hands on the back of the pew before me and gripped it. Waited for Father to speak again.

Then he put his hands up in the air and looked toward the ceiling as his mouth moved in a strange sort of whisper. I couldn't understand what he was saying or to whom he was saying it. Then it seemed as though a great shaft of light spilled in from the long window behind the rostrum and covered Father as though he were standing under a waterfall and being bathed by its powerful spray. Some of the congregants moved to their knees and clasped their hands together in prayer, a couple of the women were crying, and a few men were standing up as if about to approach the pulpit to offer Father a hand, in case he fell down under that immense light that was spilling in behind him.

Then he spoke: "My brothers and sisters," he said again. "My children." This was the first time he had called us his children, and his voice had returned to that slow and soothing tone, like someone gently running a bow across the strings of a perfectly tuned violin. "When I was about fourteen or fifteen years old," he said, "I was living in a foster home not very far from here. In Bogalusa. I had already been in and out of juvenile hall. I was a troubled boy. You must remember that. My mother had been dead for several years, and I had never even known my father, as he left us when I was just an infant. I'd eventually come to forgive him for this, but when I was a young man, I held anger in my heart. Satan had his grip on me, and I didn't even know it at the time. That's how deceitful he can be.

"There were other kids living there too, of course. Neglected or abandoned children who had also become wards of the state like myself. They lived in the same foster home and ranged in age from two years old all the way up to seventeen. Our foster parents were decent folks. People of God. Like you. They brought us to church once a week—though I didn't heed its message then—and they made sure we went to school and had food in our stomachs. I really had nothing to complain about, my sons and daughters, brothers and sisters, but as I've said, the devil had his fingers clenched tightly around my heart, and he wasn't ready to unfasten them yet. I came to learn that he would never be ready. He wanted to see if he could use me. And I didn't know him well enough back then to even put up a fight. In fact, I wouldn't have even been able to tell you at that time in my life that I was in a fight at all. My soul was being wrested from me and I had no idea it was even happening.

"One morning as we were eating breakfast, our foster mother

stepped out of the kitchen to finish getting dressed for work. She left her purse on the counter and as I looked up from my eggs and grits, I saw that her purse was partway open and there was money sticking out. It wasn't much—just a couple of twenties, a few tens. Maybe seventy dollars altogether. But I knew then that I had to have that money. I didn't know what I would do with it but something on my heart was telling me to take at least one of those bills. Just one to see if I could get away with it. So I stood up and went to the sink to scrape my plate and when I was sure the other kids weren't looking at me, I swiped one of the twenties from the purse.

"If our foster mom ever noticed the missing twenty, she never mentioned it. And I can't even tell you now what I used it on. But that's not the point of this little story, my children. The point is that I had allowed Satan to tighten his grip on me just a little bit more than he already had and by stealing that money and getting away with it, I had unknowingly opened a door to further sin. Deeper troubles.

"So was this my greatest sin?" Father asked us. "Is this the story I promised would shock you? That I stole a little bit of money from my foster mother's purse? Hasn't each one of us done something—or thought about doing something—similar? Aren't we all guilty of some sin, no matter how trivial it may seem? But what is the point? Why am I telling you this?

"I'm telling you this because a sin is like a brick. You take one and you might not have much. Just one block. You can walk over it or around it. You might not even notice it if it's in a patch of high grass. But add two or three more and you start to have something more noticeable. A few more and a few more and before you know it you have a wall. A wall of sin. And you can't get over it or around it now. It's blocking out the light in front of you. It's blocking your path. It's keeping out the people you love and keeping you trapped and alone on the other side of it.

"I'm here to tell you that this is how it works. And when you're inside the confines of that wall, the only company you have, the only solace other than your own mangled heart, is that of the beast whose fingers are still clenched tightly over you, his chains pulling harder and harder as though you were his very own marionette doll strung up and dancing for all to see.

"Children, I'm here to tell you that I was once inside this wall—and that it was of my own making. It surrounded me on all sides and I didn't have the tools with which to knock it down. So I kept building it higher and higher with sin. And this is what I started off wanting to tell you. This is what the Lord has put on me to share with you today. Open your hearts and brace your spirits:

"My dear sweet children, I—your Father, your loving shepherd, your protector, righteous in all that I believe and say—have . . . killed someone."

When Father said these words, there was an audible gasp among the congregants. I looked over at my parents and could see the look of confusion on both of their faces. Then I looked around the small church room to see what the others' reactions were. Some people were whispering to each other, a couple of the younger girls were crying, and one man was shaking his head as if he wanted to knock out of his ear and onto the floor the words he had just heard so that he could push them under the pew with his foot. Despite all this no one left.

"Now, children," Father continued, his voice still deep and strong, but with the slightest hint of a quiver underneath it, like a single minnow disturbing an otherwise smooth puddle of water. "I'm not telling you this for you to forgive me. I've already received forgiveness from our Dear Lord, and I have peace in my heart thanks to His divine mercy and everlasting love. I'm not telling you this, either, so that you feel as though you have to make a choice about whether or not you want to stay with me. You will know on your own: your decision is written on your hearts already, and God knows what it is.

"So I will tell you about what I did as a young boy, how I took the life of another boy not much older than I was at the time, in hopes that you will then open your hearts to me as well, and so that we can commune with one another, purely, as the Lord intends."

Here Father paused and looked around the sanctuary. He seemed to digest all of us with his eyes. It was as if he could almost sense the barometric pressure of the room, using his hands as they gripped the side of the dais to gauge the energy and react to it accordingly. Then I watched as he closed his black leather Bible and looked down at its cracked cover for a moment, rubbed his fingers across its surface. Contemplating.

Then he spoke:

"I was serving time in the Florida Parishes Juvenile Detention Center," he said, "for theft, which I've told you about. I was regularly attacked by the other boys there, for I was much smaller than they were, and I was a prime target. This I've also told you. I fought back when I could, and sometimes I would emerge victorious while other times I would not. I believe I've told you all of these things before, children, but what I have not shared with you yet is how I killed one of these boys during what started off as a minor scuffle in the shower. His name was Billy Milgrew.

"By that point, I had been in juvenile hall off and on for about a year and a half, and I had grown accustomed to almost daily attacks from the other boys. I knew Billy had had his eyes on me for a while and I felt that any day something was going to happen. Then one day it finally did."

At this point, Father stopped again and looked around at his congregation. He looked at all of us. One by one it seemed. He was breathing heavily, as though he had just carried a large crate up the aisle and placed it next to him at the dais. Then he bent his head down as if in prayer and continued with his confession: "I was coming out of the shower, had just wrapped a towel around myself, when this boy Billy Milgrew came up behind me and shoved me hard. The cement floor was wet and slick under my bare feet, but something—a miracle, maybe it was fate—kept me from falling, kept me from slipping. When I turned around, I instinctively knew I had to hit him back, and quickly, in order to save face with the other boys who were now watching us to see what would happen. I remember the steam in the locker room where some of the other boys were getting dressed and I remember Billy almost smiling at me as I turned to face him, as though this gave him great joy, this confrontation.

"But now I think he was just a bit shocked that I hadn't fallen down on the wet floor, because when I reached out to push him back, he didn't even lift his arms up to block. Instead, his eyes widened as his own feet began to come up from under him as he slipped on the slick concrete. Children, this was what you would have called a one-in-a-million occurrence, one of those things you could never repeat, even if your very life depended on it. That's why I think now that it was Fate putting her hand on me that day, her way of stepping into my life, for it would never be the same after that moment.

"Time seemed to slow down then and I remember watching Billy fall backward as his arms pinwheeled on either side of him and his feet came up to what seemed to be shoulder level—all of this happening in less than a second, really, but it felt as though we were moving inside of a jar filled with melted wax. When Billy landed finally, his head hit the tiled wall behind him and bent forward in a way I have never seen a human head bend before."

At this, I felt my mother's hands covering my ears, but then my dad gently pulled them off and just hugged my mother toward him and into his arms, saying, "It's okay. We need to hear this. So does the boy." My mother looked at me and then nodded back toward the dais with her chin so that I would look that way too and listen to the rest of Father's story.

Some other people in the congregation must have been doing something similar at first—turning away or shuddering under the image that had just been painted in their heads—because Father stopped speaking for a moment and looked out into the pews again. Then he closed his eyes and took another one of those exhausted breaths into his lungs. I could see his chest expanding as he sucked in the air.

"I will spare you the rest of the gory details," Father said. "But I will tell you that as soon as that stream of dark blood started coming from Billy's right ear, I knew that I had killed him. The other boys just stood there, stock still and silent. There wasn't the usual jeering that occurred during a regular fistfight. This was more serious than that. They knew it, those boys, and so did I. I don't think anyone knew what to do. I could already hear the tumbrel wheels creaking in my head as the guards led me to my death. I was finished. This is how it would end, I thought to myself. I had put the final brick in place and now I would suffocate in my chamber of sin, which I had built with my own hands.

"But that didn't happen, children. What happened was that the other boys told a story of Billy Milgrew slipping as he was coming from the shower. They said he just slid on the wet cement, that he must have walked over a smear of soap on the floor, that he'd broken his neck when he fell against the wall. I agreed with their story when it was my turn to talk, and the guards seemed to believe us, for they never pressured anyone for more information. I'm sure now that they just wanted to put this all behind them as quickly as possible in order to avoid any lawsuits or worse, losing their jobs.

"Over the years, children, I even started to believe this story myself. I was not a killer, a murderer, I told myself. I surely couldn't have done such a thing. It really was a freak accident. Yet little did I know, the devil's grip was getting tighter and tighter, like one of those vices we have over in the woodshop. Only this vice wasn't holding two broken pieces of wood together as the glue between them dries and hardens. This vice was squeezing until what was between it—my heart—would burst wide open and die the death of a thousand sinners.

"I have to confess, though, that my time in juvenile hall got a lot easier after that. None of the other boys bothered me anymore. They looked at me with respect. They stepped aside when I walked past them. And this altogether new feeling was one I quickly grew accustomed to. I was in love with being respected. It took me many years, however, to realize that it was fear that motivated those other boys, and not love. And what I was searching for then—and what all of us are searching for, are all in need of—is to just be loved. I finally found that in our Lord Jesus Christ. And now it is my mission to share that love with you. Like the song says, I once was a wretch, brothers and sisters, but now I am found! A-men!"

Some of the women were crying as Father spoke these last words. Father himself looked exhausted, as though the telling of this story took a great deal from him. Sweat was beaded up around his hairline and above his upper lip, making his thick mustache glisten in the light. He wiped his face again with his sleeve and someone brought him some water. Then Father sat down in one of the metal chairs on the stage and drank slowly from the glass, breathing heavily between sips.

No one left Father or his church that day, or even in the days and weeks and months that followed. The church actually started to grow in spite of Father's confession. Or maybe it was because of it.

Either way, by year's end our congregation had doubled, and Father was talking about building a new sanctuary. The love that everyone had for him then seemed stronger than ever, and Father appeared to be the most incredible man they had ever known. My parents said that he was a true miracle in the flesh. I still hadn't completely bought it though. But I was trying.

4

The land Father had purchased before my parents and I had even met him, which we were now helping to slowly clear out, was about forty acres all told. Its perimeter was surrounded by thick pine woods so that if you were passing on the highway, you would never know it was back there. You could still see the church from the road, though, but nothing else of what we were building in the woods.

Over a year's time, we had made two large vegetable gardens where we grew corn, tomatoes, squash, carrots, potatoes, greens, and anything else we could get to take hold there in the hard soil. We had a small orchard of peach trees, a couple of fig trees, blueberry bushes, and a few small greenhouses where we grew aloe vera, thyme, parsley, and other herbs. Father had used a backhoe to dig a well that provided clear cold water, and we also had a couple of free roaming cows, chickens, ducks, goats, pigs, and horses.

In time, there was also a barn with several stalls, a hayrick, a loft, and a silo off to the side where we kept our grain. Father had purchased a couple of four-wheelers too, which we kept on the property to make it easier to get from one end to the other, and there were also several tractors with Bush Hogs that we used to keep the land clear. It was enough to rival Mr. Tally's farm and almost any other ones in town as well. But hardly anyone knew of its existence. Which was crucial, Father said, to our success.

The congregants lived in small, pop-up camper trailers and converted school buses, which Father had finally purchased from a dealer in Picayune, Mississippi. All of the buses and campers were strategically fanned out around Father's living quarters—which consisted of two conjoined school buses that had been painted white, sliced apart, and then welded back together, forming a sort of cross. This was placed right in the center of everything so that he could look out over his dominion whenever he wanted.

For anyone flying overhead, it all must have looked quite strange: a saucer of land with a large white cross at its center, strands of clothesline and electrical cords stretched from one to the other as if it were a giant spider's web in the middle of the woods.

The buses had all been painted various colors and some of them had been connected together end to end, depending on how large the families that occupied them were. Their tires had been removed and were also painted, but pocked the land at various places and serving as planters, little red and white and pink flowers blooming now from those once-ugly rubber and steel circles.

In the beginning, Father worked in the fields with us. We watched him dangle from the freshly sawn beams of the barn roof, saw him standing under a spray of blue-white sparks as he welded off the backs of school buses, one by one, so that he could later work up another weld to attach them all back together. His muscles seemed to grow more taut each day as he carried wood, bales of hay, dug trenches for electrical lines and pipes for water distribution, tilled the gardens, cut down trees and macheted the tangled overgrowth. We helped too, of course, but it often seemed then that Father took on most of the activity as everything started to come together in those first years. It all happened so quickly it seemed impossible to keep up. Every day was something new.

One particularly long morning after working in the garden and then pulling underbrush from around the perimeter of the Acre and finally burning what seemed to be pile after pile of trash, sweating to the point of what felt like complete exhaustion, I went to the edge of the clearing and leaned against the bole of a large oak tree, scooting under the shade of its thickly leaved branches as though I were sliding beneath a crisp, cool bedsheet.

I opened my canteen and drank from it. The water tasted metallic, but it was cold and felt good going down my parched throat. Then I poured some of the water over the top of my head and let it run down the sides of my face and into the collar of my shirt. I closed my eyes and leaned deeper into the pocket of the tree trunk, its roots like someone's legs wrapped around my torso.

Then I must have started to doze off because I didn't hear anyone approaching, but when I opened my eyes, I could see Father standing over me, his shadow floating across my body, swallowing me and the dry, dusty ground around the tree. I looked up at him and squinted my eyes against the white sky behind his looming figure. I couldn't see his face, but somehow I could tell he was smiling down at me. Something warm seemed to radiate from him, like a fire stoked with large branches, their undersides white and cracked with heat as the flames ticked and popped and warmed the air around them.

"Hey, there, Eli," he said. Father had said very little to me over the past few months—he was so busy, like the rest of us—and I found myself somewhat surprised at the sound of his voice. It sounded different than it did in church, more earthy, but still soothing, almost hypnotic even.

"Hi, Father."

"How have you been doing, my son? Is all this work starting to get to you yet? This terrible heat?"

Even though I was exhausted, it did feel good to be working for a cause that my parents had told me was bigger than myself. To have some sort of vision. Or at least to share in Father's vision, which my parents had told me was magnificent and promised to yield many fruits—both literally and figuratively, they had said.

When I had asked them what that meant, they just told me I'd soon see. So I wasn't exactly lying when I responded, "I've been doing all right, Father. I'm a little tired, but I can stand it."

He smiled again, and this time I could see his face, as my eyes had begun to adjust to the glare behind him.

"You're a good boy," he said. "When I was your age, I would've done anything in my power to avoid manual labor like this. I could have come up with a million excuses to not pull at weeds and chop down trees. So there's much to admire in your work ethic, there really is."

I didn't say anything, but let the warmth of Father's praise wash over me like river water.

"You know what?" Father said, still smiling. "I have an idea. There's this burger joint down the road in Bogalusa," he said. "They have the best hamburgers and milkshakes I think I've ever had. I used to walk there sometimes after school when I was a kid. What do you think your parents would say if I took you with me into town and stopped to get you some lunch?"

"I don't know. They'd probably want me to stay here and keep working."

"Well, what if I told them I needed your help? I do need to go to the hardware store, and I really could use an extra set of hands. What do you say?"

"Sure. It's worth a try, I guess."

"Great," he said. "Meet me at my truck in five minutes. It's parked right by the side of the barn. I'll go talk to your parents."

"Okay. Thank you, Father."

"No, thank you, Eli," he said.

Then he turned and jogged away from me. I was shocked by the energy he had. Despite the heat and the hard work he had been doing all morning, Father was actually sprinting. I watched him move across the field with the agility of a large buck, who seemed to just float on the air gracefully, as though he weighed nothing at all.

I was equally amazed by his confidence. He hadn't even spoken to my parents yet, but he was so sure that they'd say yes without even wanting to talk to me first that he had just asked me to meet him by his truck.

I stood up and stretched, drinking the last of my canteen water, and then I pulled my shirt off and fanned it in the air as I walked across the field so that it could dry some before I got into Father's truck.

As I approached the barn, I heard chainsaws screaming against two by fours as some of the men cut them to length so that they could frame another shed or a greenhouse. Activity was everywhere, it seemed, and I couldn't find my parents among all the commotion, but I was sure that Father had known exactly where they were, and that he was talking to them right at that moment.

I could imagine my mother smiling at him, my dad looking to her for approval, seeing it in her face, and then acquiescing to Father's request to take me with him to Bogalusa. I imagined my dad taking off his thick work gloves and wiping the sweat and bits of grass from his face with his hairy arm before shaking Father's hand, their fingers interlocking for a moment as though they had come to some profound agreement.

Then I envisioned Father's eyes gleaming as he walked away from my parents, their backs bending down toward the earth again as they shoveled at the hard ground, the din of their metal blades against the dry topsoil.

Since we moved out here, my parents had become different people. My mother had stopped taking pills—I had watched her dump them into the creek one afternoon when we were out there washing clothes against an old washboard, the little pink and white capsules floating away with the current like so many stars moving across the sky—and my dad was working every day, seemed to be genuinely happy doing it, unlike his frustration at having to do anything when we lived on Mr. Tally's farm. They never fought anymore either. They were quiet now, subdued, maybe even happy.

I started walking toward the barn and to where Father's truck was parked just beside it. The glare from the tin roof was white and bounced off of the truck's windshield. I put my arm across my eyes to block off the light so that I could see if Father was there or not. He wasn't, but a couple of the men from the congregation were pulling two by fours from the large bed and placing them on the ground. Father must have already told them to unload the truck so we could leave.

Then I felt a hand on my shoulder, the fingers grasping my collarbone. Tight but not enough to hurt.

It was Father.

I couldn't see him but his shadow was again covering my own and stretching out over the ground in front of me.

I didn't say anything. Just looked at our shadows, how much larger his was than mine as it cast itself over the dust and the grass before us.

"Let's get out of here," Father said, smiling as he led me to where his truck sat sweating in the noonday sun, the men still unloading the last of the lumber like pallbearers carrying off a coffin from the churchyard and into its place of final and eternal rest.

5

As we drove down Highway 16, Father kept his window rolled open and the radio tuned low to a country music station. We were mostly quiet, the road spooling out before us like a conveyor belt dragging Father's truck across the earth. It reminded me of when my own father and I had driven down this same highway that night we had gone to the fair—back when all of this would have seemed unimaginable.

I looked over at Father.

His hair, which had grown out considerably over the past few months, blew against his neck like tendrils of flame working up the bole of a tree. His beard was starting to thicken too. Beneath it, you could still see his cheekbones, which were hard and angular, making him look more like a man of the woods than a preacher—his boots, his rough-worn jeans, his flannel shirt.

Then I looked out of my opened window and past the highway at the trees, the occasional sandpit with its glistening water nestled among them as they seemed to fight for space in that vast and crowded landscape, a chance to touch the sun and breathe from the clear blue sky overhead. It was as though everything beyond the stretch of pavement was looking for a way out from behind those lengths of rusty barbed wire fences that held them back from the road and were pocked with POSTED and NO TRESPASSING signs.

When the woods became thick and dark and there was nothing else to see, I looked ahead and counted the yellow ticks in the center of the highway, watched how they almost transformed into a single straight line as we approached a crest in the road, then turned back to small bright slashes, broken apart only by the little orange reflectors that were stamped between them.

Father looked over at me, seemed to notice me staring at the lines in the road as though I were watching a reel of film unroll across the surface of his windshield.

"Eli," he said. "Do you know why some of the lines are dashes like that and sometimes they're just straight and solid lines?"

"No," I said.

"Your parents never taught you about that?"

"No."

"Well, basically, if you see dashes in the middle of the road—like that," he said, pointing in front of us. "That means you can pass the car in front of you. If there's a straight line—or double straight lines—that means no one can pass. Make sense?"

"Yes," I said, watching again the solid yellow lines as we approached the rise of a hill, how they afterward broke up into dashes again as we descended on the other side of the crest and the road grew flat again. It was as if we were in a boat, riding the swells of an ocean.

"Now speaking of driving," Father continued, "if you ever get lost, one thing you can do is look at the number of the road you're on. Take this road, for example," he said. "This is Highway 16, right?"

"Yes."

"Well, sixteen's an even number. All even-numbered roads go either east or west. So if you're on a road with an even number, you can narrow down the direction you're going by half. That gives you a fifty-fifty shot at getting to wherever it is that you're trying to go. Make sense?"

"Yes," I said again. My parents had never taught me about these sorts of practical details. They thought they were pointless. But here was a man who my parents respected tremendously, and he knew these things. Thought them important enough to share with me. It may have been pointless, but it was a way of organizing the world, making sense out of things that didn't otherwise make sense.

"And so odd-numbered roads go north and south?" I asked, just so Father knew I was listening and understood the simple lesson he was teaching me.

"That's right. See, the people who built this country didn't do everything wrong, did they?"

"No," I said.

"I'm telling you all of these things, Eli, because I never had anyone to tell them to me. I never had a father—or a mother—as you know. I was an orphan from day one. No one wanted me, so I became a child of the world. At least that's how I like to think of myself now. Do you ever read comic books, Eli?"

Immediately I thought of the comic strip I had drawn for the Just Say No contest, but I couldn't imagine how Father could've known about that. "Not really," I said. "My parents wouldn't let me look at things like that."

"Well, that's understandable," he said. "All the violence. Magic and spells. I could see how those books could be perceived as being evil. But you do know about Superman and Spiderman and guys like that, right? Batman?"

"Yes," I said. Despite my parents' efforts to shield me from all the secular things in the world, I had at least managed to hear of some things.

"Well they were all orphans, you know? Then they sort of became adopted by the entire world. Became heroes that everyone else looked to for comfort and safety. I know those are fictional stories, but I like that idea, don't you? It's like you make a sacrifice—the ultimate one of losing your parents—but then everyone else sort of adopts you. Kind of makes being an orphan a little more palatable. I don't know. At least it does to me."

I didn't say anything, just tried to think about what Father was telling me—and why—as I stared out of the windshield, the truck putting more of the highway behind us each minute.

Then he continued: "Sometimes I like to think of myself as one of those heroes," he said. "Here to save the world from evil. I hope you don't think that's dumb."

"I don't," I said. "I think it's cool."

"Good," Father said. "I'm glad."

In some ways, Father was the person I had always wished for in my own parents. He was a man of compassion and patience. Understanding. Depth. But there was more than that. When you were with him, it was as though no one else in the world existed but you. Even then I knew that very few people in the world could make you feel that way. And even though I sometimes questioned the things Father did in church, the stories he told, I felt lucky to be in his presence. And I understood that those were details he had used just to illustrate a point—a means to an end. It didn't all have to be true for me to believe it.

After a few more minutes of driving, Father put his hand on the radio knob and clicked it off. Then he downshifted and started to slow the truck against a rise as we came into the city. From where I was sitting in the cab, I could see a tendril of thick, white smoke being belched from the smokestacks of the looming paper mill, which seemed to hover over the town like the dark shadow of a raincloud. The smoke gusted up from behind the tree line and the buildings like the constant exhalations from an old man's pipe.

"You see that?" Father asked, watching me out of his peripheral vision as I stared at the wide metal chimneys jutting up into the sky.

"Yes," I said. The wind rushed through the cab of the truck, but had quieted a bit as Father slowed down and as we rolled under an old train trestle covered with rust and graffiti.

"That's the International Paper Mill. I used to work there when

I was younger. Twelve hour shifts every day. You think working on the Acre is hard, now let me tell you: that was hard work."

I thought about what that must have been like. Tried to imagine Father in the confines of that mill. The noise, the smell of burning chemicals in your nose. The buzzing fluorescent lights overhead, never being able to distinguish night from day while you worked inside of that windowless cavern of machinery.

Based on how it looked from the outside—its white-and-tan steel facade, connected by what seemed to be miles of planks and railed staircases going up to countless well-towers and then down into the bowels of the mill itself, the black-and-red stenciled letters of caution, warning workers of the overhead clearances, the distance from the gangplanks to the hard concrete beneath—I couldn't begin to imagine what it must have been like to spend twelve hours a day inside of a place like that. Seeing it all just made me like and respect Father that much more.

He was looking at me, seemed to notice that I was processing all of this sensory information, because then he said, "Smells horrible out here, doesn't it? And to think people live with this stench all the time. That's partly why I love the country where we are now so much. Fresh air is almost a commodity these days, Eli."

I kept looking out of my window as we passed scores of dilapidated buildings, their overgrown yards, the boarded-up windows. The neighborhoods were occasionally pocked with a couple of small clapboard houses as well, dirty and shirtless children playing on broken bicycles or wading in small plastic pools nestled among the weeds.

"It's sad, isn't it?" Father said as we came to a stop sign. He clicked on his turning light and eased the truck up a small rise. "This place used to be prosperous, you know? A whole city built up around a lumber mill.

"Believe it or not, there was tons of money here once. Mansions. A train station. A resort overlooking a man-made lake. They called it the Magic City because it grew so fast. Now look at it."

I watched as Father drove us past house after abandoned house. For Sale signs leaned grotesquely in each of the yards, but like the houses themselves, the signs looked forlorn and foreboding. Weeds came up as high as the placards, covering the realtors' names and contact information. It didn't seem to matter, though. No one was buying any of these houses anyway.

"Do you know that 'Bogalusa' is a Choctaw word?" Father said, pulling my attention back into the cab of the truck. "It means 'dark water.' Seems appropriate, doesn't it? When you drive through here like this, it really does seem like there's something dark flowing through the veins of this place. Like the city's haunted. Do you ever think about stuff like that, Eli?"

"Stuff like what?" I said.

"I don't know. Energy. Spiritual vibes in a certain place. I know the Bible tells us not to dwell in these things, but I can't help but wonder about them when I come out here. How a place could become so hollow, so dead. Yet still exist physically. It happens to people all the time, but an entire place? I don't know. It's just fascinating to me. It makes me kind of sad too."

It was hard to know what to say so I just stayed quiet and tried to take everything in that Father was telling me. It seemed as if there was something I was supposed to be learning from this so I just concentrated like I was in church and listening to one of his sermons. Even though this was much different, more personal, tactile somehow.

Father continued to navigate his truck up and down the circuitous roads, which all seemed to emanate from the paper mill, that steel hulk in the middle of a dead city, constantly chuffing out plumes of thick, white, sulfuric-smelling smoke.

"Well," Father was saying as we continued to drive, "I thought about these things a lot over the years. You know, after my mother died and I was moved from foster home to foster home, then to juvenile detention center, I thought a lot about how different places had certain energies about them—some good, some bad. I could never put my finger on what this was, though, what to attribute it to. And it wasn't until I discovered the Scripture that I got my answer."

Father looked over at me and seemed to wait for what he was saying to sink in. Then he said, "Now it just seems so simple that I feel stupid for not recognizing it before. It's about God and Satan. Good and evil.

"See," he said. "When people start to let Satan into their homes, he takes over, spreads like a disease. It starts off small, like those bricks of sin I talked about before in church. But after a while, it all adds up and before you know it, he's taken over. You can see that here, in this town, if you just look at its history.

"This place was built on the destruction of the land, of God's resources: His trees and waterways. Then came the money. People couldn't get enough of it. It was their drug. They worshiped it. They cut down more trees, built more buildings, lavished their surroundings to show off what they had. There's nothing magic about that, Eli. It's evil. Plain and simple."

As Father spoke, then stopped, it was almost as though I was floating through a vat of petroleum jelly as I listened to him. Everything became slow, sounds were muffled, the windshield blurry. It was as if I were under a spell. Dreaming. Father's words had always affected me—from the first time I heard him speak in church—but this was different. More intense. I glanced over at him. He was looking partway out the window as he drove, the breeze coming through and blowing his hair across his shoulders.

Then I looked ahead and leaned back into my seat, still listening. Father continued, "Did I ever tell you that my people were Choctaw, Eli? That they settled on the Pearl River in what's now called Talisheek? That's their word for gravel or small pebbles. I'll have to take you there sometime—yet one more little town around here with some interesting history and energy in it. Something you'd have to feel for yourself to know what I'm talking about.

"Anyway, when the white folks started settling here, though, they tried to convert my people. Thought they were heathens. Nature-worshipers. But all this did was lead to violence. When I was very young, my mother used to tell me stories about how the European settlers would get sick and die of malaria or some other horrible disease, and then they would give the blankets from their dead—the ones that the sick people had died in—to the Indians. It was like their own Trojan horse. Do you know that story?"

I looked across the cab at Father. "Yes," I said. "I read about that before. How all those soldiers hid inside of a big wooden horse, then after it was wheeled into this walled city, they came out and killed everyone."

Father smiled. "Yeah, that's pretty much right. That's what the white people who came here did to the Indians. My people. They wouldn't convert to this new belief system, nor would they give up their land, so these new settlers basically killed them off. Moved them into little condensed pockets of earth where they could be controlled like cattle and then exterminated. Only they probably treated their cattle better than those poor people.

"It was an unspeakable thing, Eli. But we can't forget it happened. Even if we wanted to, this place won't let us. Just look around you. I really think that's how the evil started to gain its traction here. It was the first brick, so to speak. It may have been disguised for a while by this town's prosperity, but that's exactly how Satan works. With smoke and mirrors.

"Of course, you could say the first real brick in the wall here was my people's unfamiliarity with Jesus, His teachings. You could say that's what led to the violence and all the evil that followed. But I don't believe that. I think my people were holy. They were truth-seekers, like me, and they were at the right hand of the Lord. They just didn't know Him in the so-called traditional way that we do now. But that doesn't matter. It was a different incarnation they were familiar with. Our savior, I believe, is universal—He transcends all faiths and understandings.

"The point of all this, Eli, is just to say that places like this are infected, like those malaria-soaked blankets, and until you get rid of the disease at its source, everyone living here will be sick. They'll die, both spiritually and physically. And it can happen to entire places just as easily as it can to individual people. The only way to disinfect yourself is with Jesus's blood. But the good news is that He's already offered it to us when they nailed him up on that cross. We just have to accept it.

"My dream, Eli, is to one day get this whole city to see that—to accept the Lord and kick Satan right out of here. Who knows how wide it can spread? We might be able to tell all the world about it. Does that sound good to you?"

"Yes," I said.

"Wonderful," Father said. "Now enough of that. Are you hungry?"

"A little bit."

"Good, because I'm starving," Father said.

6

We pulled up at the old Zesto Drive-In on Richmond Street and Father parked his truck in the empty asphalt lot.

The restaurant was in an old brick building, low-ceilinged and flat, with a large metal rooster on the roof. The rooster looked to be at least six feet tall and it had rivulets of orange rust dripping down its faded white neck and wings, almost covering its long, pencil-yellow legs and feet. It had a green tail and its beak was pointed toward the sign in front of it, which was also metal, but painted blue and with the word ZESTO scripted across it in bright yellow as though the word were itself a fast-moving glacier.

Just beyond that there was a giant metal ice-cream cone, with a swirl of dirt-smeared soft-serve emerging from it and leaning toward the front of the building. Several thick black power lines snaked out from the transformer on the creosote-covered electrical pole next to the street, the wires traveling into the rusty sign like veins.

"Come on," Father said, smiling over at me as I took everything in. The vinyl seat creaked under him as he slid from the cab. Then he grabbed his wallet from atop the cracked dashboard where it had sat baking in the sun while we were driving. He slid it into the back pocket of his jeans.

As I climbed out of Father's truck and started to walk across the gravel-and-asphalt lot, I could hear some sort of commotion behind the restaurant, just between the squat building and the dilapidated fence that blocked it off from the Magic City Auto

Works next door. It sounded like someone was pounding on a sheet of tin with their boots, but then I heard a man's voice crying out, and Father started walking toward the sound.

Quickly.

I followed him.

Just next to a pile of discarded tires I saw four or five men surrounding another man, who was thin and weak-looking. They were pushing him around as though he were a pinball bouncing back and forth in a plastic bucket. I shuddered each time they pushed him against that sheet metal wall and heard him grunt in pain, but the men just laughed as I stood there watching, helpless and scared. Then Father started walking up to them.

"Can I help you?" one of the men said after he noticed Father approaching.

"I'm not sure yet," Father said. Calmly. As though he were delivering one of his sermons in church.

"Well, then maybe you should mind your own damned business," the man said, looking toward his friend and laughing.

"I think this is my business, brother."

"I ain't your fuckin' brother, hoss. Now why don't you take your little boy and get the fuck outta here."

The other two laughed, then pushed the skinny man back up against the sheet metal. It thudded behind him and I could hear him grunt again as his back hit its corrugated surface. Then they thrust him over and into a pile of greasy tires. When he tried to stand, one of the men pushed him back down with his dirty boot, leaving a dark-gray tread mark across his jeans. They all laughed.

"That's enough," Father said. "Leave him alone."

"Fuck off," one of the men said, sticking his middle finger out at Father, who lifted the leg of his jeans up so that they could see his boot and what he had tucked inside of it. Then he unsnapped the sheath that was strapped against his calf and slid out a knife. It looked almost identical to the one I had gotten at the fair. I hadn't seen that knife since my dad had used it to slash Mr. Tally's tires that night, and I wondered if it could've actually been mine as Father held it out before him and the sunlight glinted off its metal blade.

Things started to move faster then, and next thing I knew Father was holding one of the men by his shirt, the knife blade pressed against the man's throat. A trickle of blood formed dark and bulbous at the tip of the blade, and the man's eyes seemed to grow inside of his grizzled face. His friends just stood there frozen, as though Father had paralyzed both of them. It was like watching what he had done to Leon back at church: the electricity that seemed to emanate from his hands, the ions floating in the air like particles in lake water.

Father held the knife against the man's throat, kept his body pressed tight against him like he was performing a wrestling move. "Next time," he said, "the Lord may not be so merciful on you, brother." Then he took the knife and made a small slit on the surface of the man's skin, just under his jawbone where the flesh was soft and vulnerable. The man winced, sucked in air through his partially closed mouth. Father said to him, "Now you just consider yourself lucky it was me who found you, or this could've been a lot worse."

The other two men stood there for a second, watching, then ran off across the parking lot and disappeared into the dark, murmuring pines beyond the fence line.

Then Father pushed the man away from him, who stumbled forward and grabbed at his neck, looking up at Father and breathing heavily. Blood trickled through his fingers. He pulled his hand away and looked at it.

"You cut me, man," he said. "What the hell is the matter with you?"

Father didn't answer him, just shooed him away with his hand, as he would a dog. The man looked at him for a second, then back at his bloody fingertips. Then he stumbled across the hot asphalt lot and disappeared into the woods where his friends had gone.

I watched the trees as they seemed to swallow him up, like something out of a Grimm's fairy tale.

Father looked at me, then sheathed his knife and pulled his jeans back over his boots. He had a slight smile on his face, and I started to think about the story he had told us about the boy he killed in juvenile hall. I didn't know if what he just did was good or bad. "Are you okay?" he said.

"Yes."

"Good. I'm sorry you had to see that, Eli."

I didn't say anything.

On the ground, the man who had been beaten up was still trying to catch his breath. His arms and his shirt were stained gray-black from the dirty tires and the other men's boots.

His face was sweaty, streaked with oily black smudges, and he was breathing heavily. I could hear his shoes scraping at the small pieces of gravel in the lot around him as he tried to find purchase on the ground.

"Here, let me help you," Father said, bending down to offer his hand. "Are you okay, brother?"

"Yeah, I'll be all right."

"Do you think you're okay to stand up?"

"I hope so. It feels like they broke my damn ribs."

"Eli," Father said, looking back to where I was still standing. "Come around and help me stand him up."

I did what he told me.

Once the man was on his feet, Father asked him his name. "It's Paul," the man said.

"Like the disciple," Father said, nodding, as though speaking to himself. "That's a wonderful name." Then he asked, "Do you know why those men were hurting you like that?"

"No. All I did was ask if they had any spare change so I could get something to eat. They laughed at me. One of 'em spit in my face. As soon as I started walking away, they jumped me."

Father looked at him, slowly shaking his head. Then he looked out at the parking lot and the dark woods beyond it where the other men had disappeared.

"Are you hungry?" Father finally asked.

"Yes, sir," Paul said through his heavy breathing. "Very much so."

"Well, we were just about to get some hamburgers. You're welcome to join us."

"Oh, thank you," Paul said. "God bless you and your boy." He was looking at me now and smiling. I didn't want to tell him that Father was not actually my dad. Though I sort of liked the idea that he could've been just then. That this man Paul actually thought he was made me feel good, part of something special. Especially after witnessing what Father had just done to help him.

"Thanks," Father said. "But this young man isn't my son. His name's Eli. He's a good kid. He and his parents live with me and some other folks out on some land we all share not too far from here, in Angie.

"Maybe you'd like to come back there with us? We can give you a place to sleep and some food. Once you're healed up, we could really use the extra set of hands too. I'm not gonna lie to you: I think this is no accident that we met today, Paul. Though I do realize the circumstances weren't ideal." Father smiled again. "The Lord does work in mysterious ways," he said.

Paul looked at Father for a minute, seemed to consider his offer of shelter and food, how it probably seemed too good to be true. He was most likely wondering how his luck could have changed that quickly. He had gone from being jumped by three other men just a couple of minutes earlier to being offered food and a place to live.

But that was how things were with Father. And if this man Paul had any reservations at all about him—how quickly and instinctively he had pulled out that knife and had cut another man, sending him running with his friends into the woods, leaning into the very act of violence as naturally as someone taking a breath—my simple presence alone was probably enough to assuage them.

Paul looked around the empty parking lot then down at me. "Okay," he said.

After Father ordered and paid for our food, the three of us sat in the shade at one of the warped picnic tables and ate our hamburgers.

I thought about my parents, how they would have once called this food poison, but since living on the Acre with Father, had started to give up so many of their old convictions. They had grown quiet, busy with the physical labors that left them tired and subdued by the end of the day. I hardly saw them anymore, it seemed. Sometimes I even missed them.

I sat there listening to Father talk to Paul. Occasionally, I looked down at my paper hamburger tray, which was soggy with thick mounds of ketchup and French fries, and I ate the burger Father had gotten for me, its gobs of mustard and mayonnaise and pickles, its pieces of shredded cheese dripping down onto my lap and the wooden surface of the table.

Father was telling Paul about the Acre and the work we were doing there. How important it was to belong to a community. Paul just nodded and ate, not even bothering to wipe the ketchup from his lips as he shoved the food into his mouth.

Father just kept talking. And when Paul finished his hamburger and his fries and had dabbed up all the ketchup from his tray with his fingers and had licked them clean, Father smiled at him and then slid his own uneaten food across the table toward Paul, nodded that he should eat it too. So he did. Taking sips of root beer from a Styrofoam cup filled with pebbled ice to wash it all down.

Like Paul I just listened and ate until it was time to go.

7

When we got back to the Acre, Father told Paul to go into the church and that someone there would bandage him up and show him a cot he could rest on. Father said that he'd be there in a little while to check on him. Then we watched Paul as he limped away across the field. I wondered why Father hadn't just healed him like he had done with that man Leon, why he had brought him back here to the Acre, only to send him away like that.

"Well," Father was saying, "this sure turned out to be an interesting afternoon, didn't it?"

"Yes," I said.

"I'm glad we got to talk a little bit, though. You're a bright kid, Eli."

"Thanks, Father. And thank you for lunch, too."

"That was my pleasure, Eli. A good kid like you deserves something nice every once and a while, don't you think?"

I didn't answer him, but wondered what my parents would have said to this. It seemed as if they believed I should struggle for the things I wanted out of life. That a difficult existence made you a better person. They were always worried I was going to become spoiled.

"Well, I guess we should get back to work then," Father said. "I'll see you later, okay?"

"Okay."

Then he reached out and took my hand, shook it like he had done the very first time my parents and I came to his church. But now his hand felt calloused, work-hardened, dry. Nothing like how soft it had once been. We were all changing.

A few hours later, Father called me from his bus across the field. I had been working in the garden, pulling up carrots and putting them into an old, red plastic milk crate. Everyone on the Acre had a job assigned to them and mine was to work the vegetable garden. I would walk the furrowed rows and pull up whatever was ready to be pulled, pick weeds from the soil, water it with a cracked plastic jug that leaked onto my legs.

I had to fill the jug with a hose, which was all the way next to the barn, making the trip back and forth over the hills and swales, the jug sploshing water onto my jeans and shirt, only to have the hungry soil soak it all up as soon as it was poured. Then I'd have to do it all over again.

It would take half the day sometimes but I didn't really mind. I was just happy for the distraction. When I lived on Mr. Tally's farm, there was never really much for me to do. And I knew all about idle hands. Not to mention that my parents would tell me each evening how proud they were of me now—something they had never told me before. They told me again and again how important the things we were doing here were, and how one day it would all make sense. I believed them. Or wanted to at least.

Anyway, I was hunched over pulling a carrot from the ground, dusting it off with my fingers, when I heard Father calling me. "Eli!" he was saying from the open doors of his bus, his hands cupped around his mouth so that his voice carried across the Acre and all the way to where I was working.

Some of the other congregants looked up from their chores, then shaded their eyes as they searched for me on the compound, likely wondering (as I was) what Father had wanted me for this time. I was sure they had been curious about why he had taken me to lunch, what we had talked about, who the new person was we had brought back with us. But they were all too busy to ask any questions. I knew they would later though.

I straightened myself up and put my fist in my lower back to ease the pain in my muscles from being bent over for so long. Then I put the carrot into the milk crate with the others, their green leafy stems sticking out from the diamond-shaped openings like so many fingers trying to push their way through a chain-link fence.

I picked up the crate and brought it to the edge of the garden, set it down next to some railroad ties that served as its frame. They smelled of hot tar and creosote in the sun and I could see the thick blackness of it filling the cracks of the heavy ties and oozing into the holes where the rail spikes had once been, holding them down to those endless steel tracks for God-knows how many trains to ride over, taking people from one place to the next—places I'd never been and would likely never be. A trail of ants was slowly disappearing into the space between the dirt and one of the railroad ties. I watched them go.

Then I walked across the field and toward the circle of old school buses, making my way to Father's, which sat at the center like a sun, all of the other planets orbiting around it. I had been in Father's bus only two or three times before and I couldn't imagine why he was calling me now, but figured it had something to do with what had happened earlier today.

As I walked over the grassy field, people looked up from their work and smiled at me, as though they knew something that I didn't. Father had already gone back into his bus, but I could see where he had left the doors open for me. He was waiting.

I put my right tennis shoe up onto the corrugated-rubber platform at the foot of the threshold and then knocked on the open door to let him know I was there. The door shook on its hinges and the lever that some bus driver had once likely used to open and close the door to disperse children from inside moved at the pressure of my knuckles against the glass. It was as if everything had slowed down again and I was walking through a wall of silky gauze. This was often the effect of being in Father's presence. Even anticipating it changed your perception of the world around you.

"Eli?" I heard Father call from inside. "Is that you?"

"Yes, Father," I said.

"Great, come on in. And pull those doors shut behind you, please."

"Okay," I said.

I scraped the dirt and clay from the bottoms of my tennis shoes, using the metal strip at the foot of the entrance to clean them off, then I stepped up and into the bus and pulled the lever to gentle the door shut. I could smell the vinyl seat coverings baking in the sun, the dried herbs Father had hanging from little lengths of jute twine all along the aisles. Some of the windows were open but most of them had been tinted with a film of black plastic so that inside the bus was cool and dark like a cave.

You could see the seams, like melted candlewax, where the bus had been welded into the frame of another bus, and I remember Father and some other men using a blow torch to slice the thing in half—that white spear of flame, the smell of hot steel, the sound of it. Then they had stuck them together like some strange cruciform and welded them tight.

There was music playing inside: the soft sounds of an acoustic guitar coming from the overhead speakers, an occasional river of singing undulating beneath the lulling rhythm.

"I'm back here," Father said.

I walked down the narrow aisle to reach him.

On some of the empty seats were stacks of books, musical instruments, legal tablets with Father's handwritten sermons scrawled in blue ink across their bright yellow pages. Carefully folded jeans, flannel shirts, and finally at the foot of the seat where Father was sitting, his leather work boots. I looked at them, then at his socked feet, and finally up to his face, where his blue eyes met mine and locked their focus onto me.

"Have a seat," he said, motioning to the empty bench opposite from the one where he was sitting. "I bet you didn't think we'd be talking again so soon today, huh?"

"No," I said. The vinyl creaked under my weight as I eased myself onto the bench, tufts of yellow-orange foam pushing out through a slit in the seatback, exposing a rusty metal coil.

"Sorry about that," Father said, noticing me looking at the tear. "She still needs a little bit of work."

"That's okay," I said. "It doesn't bother me."

"It's kind of like us in a way, though, isn't it? Everyone's always in need of some kind of work it seems. Whether it's spiritual or physical."

"Yeah," I said. "That's true."

I ran my hand along the seat in front of me, traced the cracks and myriad grooves with my calloused fingers, looked down at my shoes.

"Well," he continued.

I looked up. Involuntarily, it seemed, as if some magnetic force were pulling my eyes toward his. I didn't answer him, but he went on anyway.

"I wanted to give you a book, Eli," he said. "I know it's probably not what you were expecting, but I've just been thinking a lot after our trip this afternoon about how important it is for you to read. And not just the Bible, but other things too. It's so important for you to learn, Eli. And to not just work all the time."

Father stood then, squeezing himself into the narrow aisle. "Follow me," he said.

I slid out of my seat, stood, and followed him down the aisle. He stopped and looked at one of the seats, which was covered with stacks of books, hymnals, those same legal pads with his sermons written on them.

"How old are you now, Eli?" he said. "Twelve? Thirteen?"

"Fifteen," I said.

"Wow." Father smiled, shaking his head like a parent would at hearing such news. Like they can never believe how fast their kids grow up.

I could barely see his mouth beneath his thick beard, but the lines at the corners of his eyes seemed to point upward, and his cheekbones moved into the space of soft skin just under his eyes. When Father smiled, he did so with his whole face. "It's been that long, huh?" he said. "It really is amazing how fast time flies."

"Yeah."

"Well, since you're fifteen, Eli, I guess any trepidation I might have had about giving you this book was for naught then. Here."

Father bent over and reached into the stack of books and started shuffling through them. I couldn't see him so much as I could hear the pages being ruffled and a couple of books falling onto the floor under the seat.

I crouched down to try to pick them up.

"Don't worry about those," Father said. "I'll get them later."

I stood back up, leaned against the seat behind me. Waiting.

"I know it looks like a mess in here, but trust me, I know where everything is. There's a method to my madness, I promise." He smiled again, then finally stood himself.

"Here it is," he said.

Father was holding a small paperback book in his hand. He lifted it up so that it could catch some of the tinted sunlight that pierced through the half-opened window behind where he was standing. Then he turned the book so that I could see its cover. The first thing that stood out to me about it was the square of red at the bottom half, which contained what looked to be three or four stick figures, drawn hastily with a thick black marker. The figures seemed to be running, but you couldn't tell if they were running away from something or toward it.

The top half of the cover was made up of a bunch of grayish-black dots, with the title, The Outsiders, and the book's author, S. E. Hinton, written in large black lettering. The book seemed to fluoresce in the strange tinted light, which was pouring in myriad cylinders through the bus's windows and flooding the entire space where Father and I stood. He held the book before him as though it were a relic, a holy object.

I assumed that this book was some sort of religious tract, some biblical text, maybe something about a group of outcasts who were called "The Outsiders," Christians like ourselves who had been banished from their land for following Christ.

Then Father held the book closer to me, indicating that I should take it. I did. I held it there in my hand. Turned it over, thumbed through the slightly yellowed pages. He still wasn't saying anything, and I could only imagine it was because he was trying to let the moment draw itself out, the weight of it growing with each passing second. Just like he did in church when he told us something profound about himself or our unique faith and connection to the land. Then, he finally spoke again.

"I was about your age and in detention hall when I first read that book," he said. "It was the first time I read something that I felt had been written specifically for me. As though it were about me. Of course, that was before I discovered the Bible. Did you know books could do that, Eli?"

"No," I said. "What's it about?"

"Well, I want you to read it and answer that question yourself."

I flipped through the pages some more, put the book to my nose and smelled the musty paper, could even smell the glue holding the pages together. It was a wonderful scent, especially mixed with that of the drying herbs hanging from the ceiling, the cracked vinyl seats baking under the warm sun, the patchouli oil that Father fingered through his hair and beard.

It was as though all of my senses were awakened at that moment: holding the book, standing just inches apart from Father in the narrow aisle of the school bus where he lived and read and wrote, I was inspired by God to do the things he did and to say all of the things he said.

And I wondered if any of this had to do with what had happened earlier that day at lunch. If that man Paul was still here or if he had already gone. I thought about my parents too—what they would say when I told them about everything. But then, as if he were reading my thoughts, Father put his hand on my shoulder.

He said, "Now, Eli, I don't want you to tell your parents about this book. I don't think they'd understand why I gave it to you."

I didn't say anything, but instead tried to glimpse at some of the words on the pages to see if there was something scandalous printed there.

"This isn't a Christian book," Father continued. "It's a secular novel about teenagers in gangs in a small town in Oklahoma. They're rebels. But not much different from us, if you think about it."

Father turned and started inching back down the aisle toward the front of the bus. I followed him.

"Did you know that after I read that book, I wanted to be a writer?" he said.

"You did?"

"Yeah. The person who wrote it was a teenager. I thought, if she could write a book that good, then I could do something like that too. I've always written ever since."

I couldn't think of anything to say. Here Father was giving me a book, something that was not religious, and he was asking me to read it and then tell him what I thought about it. And to not mention it to anyone else.

"And all these tablets here are not just sermons I've written," Father continued, still walking down the aisle toward the front of the bus, "but stories about my childhood, my life growing up and becoming a spiritual leader. And that's really what I hope you'll do one day, Eli. Tell your story. That's why I'm giving you this book. In hopes that it will inspire you like it did with me. I can't begin to tell you how important that is in life. Being inspired."

We were at the front of the bus by then and Father sat down in the driver's seat, put his hands on the over-sized steering wheel and looked out of the windshield onto his land, which spread out before us like an ocean of grass and trees. I watched him as he pulled the metal lever to open the doors. A gust of warm air wafted in as they creaked on their rusty hinges.

"Promise me you'll read this book, Eli, and that you won't show it to anyone or tell anyone else about it. It must be our secret," he said. "I don't think some of the people here would understand why I kept that book all these years, and they especially wouldn't understand why I am giving it to you. You see, Eli, sometimes it's really difficult being in my position. People expect so much from you that they start to see you as being more than human. And while that can be a great privilege, it is also a terrible burden. Do you understand that?"

"I think so," I said.

Father just smiled again, his hand still on the metal lever, which was worn smooth by time and use.

"That's good," he said. Dreamily, as though he had just woken up from a long nap. Father was still looking out the windshield, that strange smile lifting his cheeks and creasing the corners of his eyes like sheets of crushed paper, the veined lines emanating out from a single point at the hinge of his eyelids. "Now I want you to remember to come back here and tell me what you think of that book, okay?"

"Okay," I said.

"Bye, Eli."

"Bye, Father."

I walked down the two large steps leading out of the school bus, sinking finally into the soft muddy grass at the foot of the opening. Then I put the small book in my waistband. And as I walked across the field and back to the vegetable garden, I heard the doors shut behind me, a rush of air being sucked into the bus as they smacked together—like someone taking in a deep breath before diving into a lake, the dark water closing in as you make your way to the bottom where it is cool and everything is still and quiet and peaceful.

8

When I got back to the vegetable garden, I picked up the milk crate again and started filling it with carrots. It was late afternoon and

I wanted to get my work done before it got too late and so that I might also have time to read the book Father had given to me.

My plan was to finish my work then take the book and climb into the hayloft in one of the barns to read it. Even though it would be stifling in there, with the wide bay doors open, a breeze might skirt its way in, and the shade from the stacks of hay would make it much cooler than anywhere else. Plus no one would see me, and that was probably the most important thing: keeping Father's secret.

I was sweating and could barely concentrate on the work I was doing as I went down the rows, plucking carrots from the ground and tossing them into the milk crate. Occasionally, I would feel my waistband to make sure the book was still there. It was all I could think about.

When I was finally finished combing the garden, plucking up weeds as I went, I took the milk crate full of carrots and brought it over to the side of the barn, where I used a garden hose to clean off the dirt and tiny roots that were wrapped around them. When that was done, I brought the vegetables into the barn, where someone else would slice them up and put them into one of the refrigerators we kept in there. It was a very efficient system that Father had devised early on when the Acre was first developing so that everyone shared equally in the workload.

Inside the barn was cool and shaded. It smelled of hay and also the sweet scent of horse manure, which each morning was shoveled up and taken by the wheelbarrow-full out to the compost. It would later be used in the gardens as fertilizer. Nothing on the Acre was wasted. We used everything and recycled whatever we didn't use so that it could be put to some other purpose.

Once I had set the crate of carrots—which was still dripping with the cool hosewater I had just rinsed it off with—onto one of the wooden countertops, I looked around the barn to be sure it was empty and that no one would see me climb into the loft. I could hear one of the rusty refrigerators humming next to the counter, its compressor clicking on and off as it struggled to keep its contents cold. A small window unit buzzed in the distance, blowing cool air down the muddy aisle between the horse stalls.

No horses nickered or kicked at the mud with their shod feet. There were flakes of yellow hay strewn about and I could smell its sweetness wafting up into my nose as I walked over it. I looked around again and then went over to the wooden ladder leading up into the loft. I climbed its splintered rungs, finally emerging into the darkness like someone surfacing from a cool lake and then into the heat of an afternoon summer.

The loft, as I had expected, was stiflingly hot—a few mice skittered among the bales of hay and I could see their tiny shadows seeking refuge in the far corners where the eaves of the corrugated tin roof met with the plywood floorboards. A couple of small birds fluttered nervously about the rafters, like little metal balls being smacked back and forth in a pinball machine.

When I clicked on the overhead bulb, casting a warm light throughout the space and changing the angle of shadows being thrown from the stacks of hay, I saw several more birds lift off from the beams. Another tiny mouse ticked just past my feet, still looking for shelter.

I continued walking toward the bay doors at the front of the barn, the plywood floor groaning under my steps. I held the book in my hand, careful not to bump my head on one of the rafters. When I finally got to what would have been the front of the barn, I went to the large opening that looked out onto the hills and swales of the entire Acre. From there, it was as if you were viewing an ocean from a light tower.

Two bay doors stood closed at the edge of the loft and I unlatched the rope that held them shut and carefully creaked them open, letting in some fresh warm air and a silent aspersion of dust. I kept the bit of rope loosely tied on the hasps on each door so that they wouldn't swing completely outward. I still didn't want anyone to know I was up there. If anyone happened to look up from the field, they would see me, and so I had to suffer the heat and stifled air if I wanted to read Father's book in peace.

Then I sat down in a lump of soft hay. The tiny animal noises around me had mostly died down and save for the lull of the refrigerators in the barn below and the struggling window units at the edge of the horse stalls, it was quiet. I opened the book and started reading.

Hours passed, I don't know how many, but I finished reading that book sitting there among the hay and dust in the loft. The entire time I hadn't gotten up to stretch, nor had I moved much at all as I read about those Oklahoma teenagers and the struggles of growing up poor and as outcasts in a small town where there was little hope of them ever getting out. I could understand their desperation, their dreams, their feelings of being unwanted and unloved. And while I knew, in a way, why Father had given that book to me, I was still surprised by it since it lacked any discussion of religion— unless you counted the part about watching sunsets and the Robert Frost poem they mentioned.

So what was I was supposed to think after finishing this novel Father had given to me? I didn't really know, and I was nervous because I had expected Father would ask me to tell him about it when I gave it back to him. I wouldn't know what to say. I liked the book, could see in my mind all of the things the author had described. I knew what the characters looked like, how they sounded, how it looked where they lived—even though I had never been there. I hadn't even been outside of Louisiana before.

I thought about how amazing it was that words could make pictures move inside of your head like that. It was like dreaming or watching a movie. And I felt that the least I could do for Father in return would be to tell him something profound about the story I had just read, but I just couldn't think of anything. So I opened the book again and thumbed through its yellowed pages as though there might be an answer there that I had missed the first time.

Maybe I had been so wrapped up in the story itself and what all those kids with the strange names were doing and saying that I had overlooked something. But I still couldn't make myself find it. I felt like a failure, like I was going to let Father down. I lay back in the hay and tried to think beyond what I had just read, but after a while, I decided I would just return the book to Father and apologize to him for not understanding it. Give him the chance to tell me what he wanted me to know.

As I looked out the bay doors before finally shutting them, I could see that it was getting dark. The sky had turned violet and someone had flipped on the floodlight at the front of the barn. Mosquitoes danced around in its glow and I wondered how long I had sat up there reading. How many hours had it been? I just hoped my parents wouldn't be worried.

I pulled the doors shut, put the book into my waistband, and walked through the loft, casting it into darkness as I flicked off the overhead light. Then I turned and backed down the ladder and into the barn.

9

When I got back to the middle of the field, which was sort of like walking into a giant saucer or some sort of shallow crater in the earth, people had already started to sit down for dinner. There were rows of wooden picnic tables that we kept out there, and unless it was raining or too cold outside, Father made it a point that we all ate together as a family.

People were already passing around plates of steaming chicken and corn, the bowls overflowing with fresh salads, the metal tongs for serving it sticking out from the colorful piles of lettuce and onion and tomato like a pair of antenna; there were sweating pitchers of golden brown tea or some with bright white milk, fresh from the cows we kept in our pasture; there were baskets filled with cornbread and steaming, fluffy biscuits, which were wrapped in a red-and-white checkered cloth to keep them warm. Little plates of butter, which came from the milk that we produced—churned for hours by one of the older women's calloused hands—were passed around as well, and I watched as parents knifed little yellow squares of it onto their children's plates, where it melted onto the ears of corn or into the center of a hot biscuit.

I walked over and found an empty seat next to my parents and sat down on the wooden bench. I could feel the book in my jeans and hoped it wouldn't fall out.

"Hey, Mom. Dad," I said.

"Good evening, Eli," my dad said. "Glad you could join us. Where've you been all day?"

"Nowhere," I said. "Just helping Father with some things."

"You've been spending quite a lot of time with him today, huh?" my mother said. "I'm starting to think you don't like us anymore."

"Mom," I said. "He just needs my help."

"I know, Eli," she said. "I guess I just miss you sometimes."

I didn't answer her, but instead looked over to grab the plate of food that was being passed toward me.

People were smiling and talking in hushed voices, everyone waiting for Father's arrival, which was always somewhat of a spectacle. He would emerge from his bus, sometimes wearing long flowing robes, his hair brushed and cascading down just beneath his soft shoulders, his eyes warm and glowing under the light from the setting sun, the floodlights bathing the perimeter around where we ate with their buzzing white aura. It all seemed very theatrical, but no one complained. It made every meal feel special somehow, full of meaning and significance and importance.

I took the large oval dish, which was heaped with steaming fried chicken, and put two pieces on my plate. Then I passed it over to my dad, who did the same. The rest of the dishes went around, people smiling and talking, filling up their plates with food.

When the wooden salad bowl came to me, I used the pair of metal tongs to squeeze up clumps of shiny green lettuce and bright tomatoes, all freshly picked from the garden earlier that afternoon, and I piled it all onto my plate. I hadn't realized until then how hungry I had been. I couldn't wait to eat. Now it was just a matter of waiting for Father to come out from his bus so we could start.

The dishes had made their rounds and everyone's plates were filled, including Father's at the head of the table. But we were still waiting for him to come out. Black flies hovered around the food and we swatted them away. There was a soft whispering among some of the congregants, and some of the parents of the younger children had to tell them to wait, that it would be just a couple more minutes until Father came. Then we can all eat, they said. Together.

More time passed.

There was a feeling of restlessness starting to build among the congregants as we sat there, our food cooling on our plates, the ice melting into the pitchers of tea, turning it a lighter brown as the water diluted it. Where was he?

No one seemed to want to move, probably scared to break from our tradition of watching Father emerge from his bus, robed and serene, to pray over our meal before we ate.

I looked over at my parents, who, like everyone else, were watching for Father, waiting for those doors to creak open and for him to step out onto the grass, barefoot and smiling. But nothing happened.

"Where is he?" I finally whispered.

My mother looked over at me. "I don't know, Eli," she said.

"Do you think someone should go see if he's okay?" I asked.

"Shhh," my dad told us. "Just wait. He'll come."

So I did. We all did. Waited as the sky went from a pink-orange color to mauve and then to navy as the sun disappeared first behind the black fingers of trees at the borders of the Acre and then beneath the line of the horizon altogether, until the sky was black and star-filled. Mosquitoes buzzed around us and I slapped at them on my arms and neck. Save for that no one moved. Some of the children were crying and their mothers sneaked pieces of corn bread dipped in milk into their open mouths. As though they were feeding little baby birds.

The rest of us just sat there watching the food on the table as it turned cold and untouched, everyone silent under the wash of light, which was spackled with moths and mosquitoes fluttering in its glow.

My stomach ached with hunger. I hadn't eaten since that hamburger I had with Father. And after working in the garden and then being in that hot barn loft, I was starving. I imagined that everyone else felt those same pains of hunger, which were slowly turning into worry. Concern for where Father was. Someone would have to do something.

Finally, one of the men from the congregation—I don't know who he was, there were so many of us then—stood up. "I'm going to go check on him," he said. "This ain't right. These kids are starving."

People murmured and whispered but no one else stood to go with him.

We all just watched as he walked toward Father's bus, his figure growing smaller and smaller in the light, which seemed to fade and then die away as he got farther from the picnic tables.

Father's bus was only about thirty yards away from where we sat, so we could hear as the man knocked softly on the door, then finally pried it open a little bit and called out to Father. Nothing. The man turned and looked back at us, lifted his hands up to his shoulders, palms skyward as if to signal that he didn't know where Father was.

Then someone else got up and started walking toward Father's bus. Others followed until there was a small line of people forming outside the doors leading to where Father was supposed to be but wasn't.

No one had gone in though. I could see that the inside of his bus was dark. It even felt empty somehow—like a house with a FOR SALE sign in the yard, the blinds on all the windows drawn, the yard overgrown. Like one of those houses Father and I had passed earlier that day in Bogalusa. Just looking at it you could tell that no one had lived there for a very long time.

It occurred to me then that I hadn't seen that man Paul since Father sent him into the church earlier. Did he have something to do with Father's absence? I didn't know if I should mention him or not, didn't know if anyone else even knew of his existence.

My mind was filled with the possibilities of what could be happening. After our conversation earlier, I couldn't help but think the worst. Was he dead? Had he left us? Was this a test of our loyalty to him somehow? What were we going to do if he was actually gone? Could we survive here without him? Would someone else be able to take his place, inspire us the way he had done, help us to see his vision for our lives and then accomplish it? Was there something I had missed in that book Father had given to me, something I was supposed to have seen, but didn't?

All these thoughts rushed through my head one after the other and I was no longer hungry. I pushed my plate toward the middle of the table, as though that action might set something else into motion, some movement toward another action, then something else. Something that might lead to Father's appearance. Time seemed to stop, not merely slow down like it did sometimes when Father was around, but completely halt—and I just wanted it to start again.

Now one of the men who had walked over to Father's bus and who was standing with the others just outside of it finally pulled open the doors with his hands. Then he started to walk up onto the first step leading inside. Tentatively. Then I heard him call out. "Hello?" he said. "You okay in there? Father?"

Nothing.

The man looked back at the others, several of them nodded, as if to say he should go in, and so I watched from the picnic table as his shape disappeared into the darkness. His voice sounded farther and farther away as he walked down the aisle—I could see his silhouette through several of the windows that hadn't been painted over or otherwise covered with dark sheets of curtain or pieces of plywood—turning on lights and calling out for Father.

I sat there and watched as the Emergency Exit door at the back of the bus finally flung open, and the man who had gone in to look for Father poked his head out, saying, "He's not in here."

There was an audible gasp among the congregants then, the sound of shock thrumming through the small crowd like a swell in an ocean, something that grows and grows until the water becomes too shallow and the wave finally breaks onto the shoreline. We all looked around at each other, not knowing what to do or say.

Then the man who had gone into the bus to look for Father came out of the emergency exit and walked up to the picnic tables again. Silent. Bewildered. Like the rest of us, he seemed lost and confused. In shock.

"So you mean he's gone?" a woman in the crowd asked. She was holding a small baby and rocking it back and forth in her lap.

"It looks that way," the man said.

"Well, what are we going to do now?" someone else said.

"I don't know."

People were whispering, talking to one another in hushed voices. My parents just sat on either side of me, not saying anything, their heads down, and looking resigned and defeated—like I had seen them look so many times before throughout my life.

"Come on, son," my dad said. "Let's go back inside until all this gets sorted out. There's nothing we can do about it here."

We started walking back across the field, past the picnic tables covered with plates of uneaten food and drinks, a scrim of black flies buzzing overhead. I felt at the waist of my jeans for the book Father had given to me and decided then that I should probably tell my parents about it. About the man we had helped at the hamburger place earlier. Maybe there was a connection there. Something they would notice that I hadn't yet seen.

10

About an hour or so later—after sitting in our bus in the dark, the smell of dried herbs and the soft breeze wafting up and down the aisles as I talked—my parents just sat there looking at me.

"So why do you think he told you those things, Eli?" my mother was saying.

"I don't know," I said.

My dad was sitting down thumbing through the book Father had given to me. "Have you read this before, Rebekah?" he asked my mother.

"Of course I have, John," my mother said.

"So what do you think it's all about then?"

"I don't know. None of this makes any sense." My mother put her face in her hands and shook her head.

I was glad my parents weren't arguing. Since we had moved out to the Acre, they seemed much more calm and clear-headed than they ever had before. And I was terrified that this would change if Father was really gone.

"So, Eli," my dad was saying to me now, "when Father took you to lunch earlier, was he acting strange then? Other than the fight you just told us about and that man you picked up, was there anything else that happened?"

"No," I said. "He did say something to me about how hard it was to be in his position though. How much pressure he felt."

"Well, I would say that's significant, Eli," my mother said. "What else did he say?"

"I don't know. I was thinking about the book he gave me though. How it had that poem in it. The one by Robert Frost.

"It says how everything that's gold goes away. Like sunsets and things like that. It's like nothing beautiful lasts. Maybe Father was trying to say something like that about himself. Do you think?"

My mother didn't answer me, but I could tell she was thinking about what I had just told her.

Then my dad started talking again, seeming not to have heard what I just said. "Well, what I want to know," he was saying, "is where this guy Paul is. Did Father seem like he knew him already when you picked him up today?"

"No," I said. "Not to me."

"Have you seen him before, Rebekah?"

"No, John, I haven't. How would I even know that anyway? There's literally hundreds of people here. They come and go all the time."

My dad kept flipping through the book, seeming almost angry now. Then he threw it down on the dusty aisle of our old bus and stormed outside, leaving my mother and me sitting there in the stillness, barely a breeze coming through to stir the air. I could tell that he was finished thinking about all of this. Whatever hope he had salvaged in his heart when we first moved out onto the Acre was gone again.

1

We survived. We all did. Father had disappeared from our lives and no one had ever seen that man Paul again either. A few people tried to keep the Acre going, but it just wasn't the same anymore without Father. Eventually, everyone just scattered forth into the world, tried to find their own way again.

Some of the former congregants wore their scars openly and would speak out against Father whenever they could. They were angry, they felt betrayed. It was one of the greatest lies some of them had ever been told, they said. They didn't know what to believe anymore.

My own parents stopped believing in God completely after that. They would spend their time talking about how religion was a scam, the Bible a fairy tale made up for adults. I remember how they seemed proud of this new belief, too, how they jumped into it wholeheartedly. Carried signs in front of schools, even churches, that said things like: "God isn't Dead. He never existed at all" and "Keep Christ out of Church."

It was almost as if their zeal had to be pointed in some new direction like that; otherwise, it would turn inward and they would be destroyed—by themselves or simply by the nagging thought that they had been betrayed by someone whom they loved and trusted, to whom they had given everything they owned. For them, there was nothing else left to give. Nothing but hatred and disbelief.

I just did what I had always done: I followed my parents into their new mission of disavowing God and any form of organized religion they could find. I was starting, however, to form my own thoughts and ideas about things. I had come to love Father, not so much for his religious views, but the practical things he had taught me—how to ride a bike, how to tell if an egg was hard-boiled or not, simply by spinning it around on a countertop. If the egg spun fast, Father had told me once, it was boiled. If it spun slowly, it wasn't.

When we had gone to the hardware store together one time and I had put down a pile of nails on the counter to buy for some project we had been working on, and when the man who worked there—after weighing them out and punching in some keys on the register—said, "That'll be two bits, young man," it was Father who told me what that meant.

I remember looking at the man and smiling slightly, as though I thought he was telling a joke. I had never heard that expression before. Two bits. But when he didn't smile back, I looked over at Father, who had been standing beside me the whole time.

Father never laughed or criticized me as my own dad would've probably done. He just put his hand on my shoulder and said, "He means twenty-five cents, Eli. All the old timers around here still say that." Then he winked at the man behind the counter and in that short moment was able to make both of us feel good about ourselves, as if we were a part of some secret club. These were small things, I know that, but it all meant something to me. It meant that the world could be understood, put into order.

That was Father's gift. And even though I had doubted him at first—questioning the truth of the things he had told us about his own life, his own trials, the miracles he performed—I had come to understand that if he had been lying to us then that it had been for a greater cause: so that we could experience the love and wisdom he had to share with us. Maybe it was like my mother had told me. Maybe all of the things Father said were just metaphors, something we had to really bite away at, like an apple, so that we could get to its core. I was willing to do that. I had wanted to understand that badly.

But now he was gone. And though he had left most of his clothes and books sitting inside of his bus, Father had taken the yellow legal tablets he had used to write his sermons in. No one had ever seen them again. Instead, we were all just left to pick up the pieces he had abandoned, scattered about like the tools in his woodshop.

My dad tried to get his old job back with Mr. Tally, but he had already hired someone else, was already renting the little house we used to live in to another family. Even if he hadn't though, Mr. Tally had said, after what my dad had done to him, Hell would have had to freeze over before he ever let him back onto his property again. "I can't believe you'd even have the gall to come here and ask," he had said.

But we were desperate. Scared. And so once again my parents and I lived in the back of my dad's pickup truck, parking in the woods and sleeping in its bed on frayed blankets. If the mosquitoes got too bad, my mother would sometimes spread a thin sheet out over us, and I can remember looking through it at the light from the stars and praying to a God my parents now no longer believed in that we would find a new place to live.

I so often wondered why my parents didn't just drive away from that place. Leave Louisiana altogether. After all, there was nothing really keeping us there. We had no family other than each other. We had no land, no place to live. My dad could find a job as a carpenter or a repairman or a farmhand almost anywhere. So why did we have to stay in this small town, driving back and forth on the lonely highways, my dad constantly staring at the gas gauge, hoping we could get a couple more miles in before we completely ran out and he had to ask someone for money to buy more?

Why had our lives unfolded like they had so far? Why had we been led to Father, only to have him disappear, forcing us back to where we had started? What was the metaphor of all of this? Was there one? But those were questions that no one knew the answers to. They were questions you asked yourself in the middle of the night when you couldn't sleep, when the quiet was all there was and the answers seemed a little bit farther away than they did in the daytime.

2

My dad eventually found a job and started making enough money to rent an old singlewide trailer just outside of Franklinton. I started working too. So did my mother. But my parents were tired and none of us seemed to know where to go anymore, what our purpose was in life—if it meant anything at all or if it was just a series of random events leading to nothing.

But maybe the things we do in our lives have nothing to do with chance. Maybe they've already all been written.

The St. Tammany Parish Jail. A holding cell. The guard closes the barred door behind me and I just stand there for a minute, taking in my surroundings: the four concrete walls lined with metal benches and littered with men, some of them sitting with their heads cocked over on their shoulders, sleeping. Or at least trying to. Their mouths slightly hinged open, all of them looking hung over or drunk.

A couple of men are standing in a semicircle next to the bars that front the cell, holding cigarettes out through the openings and watching as the officers walk back down the corridor to the room I had just come from, where they had fingerprinted me and had taken down all of my information. One of the men looks over at me and nods. I nod back, then walk over to the middle of the cell, where the cement floor slopes downward a bit until it ends at a metal drain cover.

There's a stainless steel toilet in the corner but it's clogged with what looks like thin blankets or sheets. The water has already overflowed into the cell and is draining through the hole in the middle of the floor, but I can still see the wet places on the ground where it hasn't gone all the way out yet. It smells like a dirty outside bathroom at the side of a bar. And someone is actually pissing on the wall.

There's no space on any of the benches, so I just stand there and wait to be taken back out to make my phone call. I don't talk to anyone. Instead, I keep my eyes focused on the dirty concrete floor or otherwise on the walls surrounding me, which are covered with graffiti and spit and piss. Names and numbers that mean nothing to me, and probably not to anyone else in here either.

There's a small TV out in the corridor and occasionally I look up at that, but I'm too afraid I might accidentally look at one of the men standing next to the bars, smoking cigarettes and yelling at the guards as they walk past. So I keep my eyes mostly on my shoes.

Then I hear an older man who is sitting on one of the metal benches on the side of the cell say, "Hey, honey." I don't look up but I'm pretty sure he's talking to me.

I had seen him when the officer first nudged me into the cell with his baton and I had quickly turned away from him after he smiled at me and blew me a kiss, his puckered lips glossy with ChapStick and his mouth slightly opened, revealing several gold teeth bordering the otherwise empty spaces where teeth once were. And before I could completely look away, he had stuck his tongue out at me, playfully. I could see a little diamond stud right in the center of it.

His nails are painted red and he has long, dry hair, black with streaks of gray, which is pulled taut against his head into a small bun at the back of his skull.

Then he says it again: "Hey, honey." This time I accidentally look at him, but only out of reflex. I can see now that he's also wearing a red sweater and tight jeans, which look to have been hacked off well above his ankles so that you can see the dark stubble on his calves. Below that he's wearing thick, white socks under a pair of orange, plastic, jail-issued flip-flops.

I look away, trying to keep my eyes on the TV, which is suspended on a metal shelf in the upper corner at the end of the corridor and playing some late-night talk show. The picture is faded and has an almost-greenish tint to it, the images flickering up and down across the tiny screen, which is made even more difficult to see with the little metal cage that covers the glass so that no one can throw anything at it and break it.

I pretend to be absorbed by the show, hoping this man will leave me alone.

But he doesn't.

"I said, Hey, honey. Ain't your mama ever teach you to speak to someone when they talkin to you?"

I still don't say anything, but a couple of guys who are standing by the bars—their arms dangling out into the corridor, flicking the ashes from their cigarettes onto the concrete floor—look up at me and sort of laugh as though they know what's coming. They've seen this before. One of them just shakes his head, then turns to look back out at the fluorescent-lit hall, glances blankly up at the TV screen as he continues to smoke his cigarette.

"Get this shit here," the man with the nail polish is saying now, but this time to no one in particular. "This boy think he too good to talk to us." Then to me again: "Is that what it is? Huh? You too good to say hi to me, cuz?"

I turn my head toward him again. He's still sitting on one of the metal benches with his legs crossed, his hands resting daintily on his thighs so that his red fingernails are on display for everyone in the cell to see.

"Sorry," I say. "I didn't know you were talking to me." It feels as if my heart is slowly beating its way into my throat. I want to throw up but close my mouth to keep it from coming right out and onto the dirty cement floor.

"That's okay, honey," the man says now. "I forgive you. Why don't you come sit down over here and make it up to me, though?" He nudges with his elbow at one of the men sitting next to him, who gets up, making room for me on the metal bench. The man with the fingernail polish pats the empty space with his hand.

"No thanks," I say. "I'm about to get out of here anyway. I'm just waiting for my phone call."

"Sugar, you're gonna be waiting a loooong time for that. I promise. Ain't none of these motherfuckers in no hurry to get your sorry ass outta here. Trust me." He smiles as he says this, as if he is giving me a piece of friendly advice, but then his smile quickly disappears from his face. It is as if someone has just flicked off a light switch. Then his bloodshot eyes narrow, seem to almost change colors. When he speaks again, his voice sounds as though it has gone down several octaves.

"Now come over here and sit the fuck down," he says. "And I ain't asking this time either, motherfucker."

I look at him. A couple of the men who are standing next to the bars shift their bodies a bit, as if preparing for a fight, but otherwise everything in the cell is still. It is as if sound has ceased and someone has stuffed wads of cotton into my ears. I can hear my heart thudding inside of my chest. I heave my breath a couple of times. I don't know what else to do. So I just start walking over to the bench, hoping one of the guards will come back before I get there.

The man who has gotten up to make room for me is smiling lecherously as I walk toward the metal bench. I look back at the cell door again, slowly, trying to buy more time, and I have the feeling like I am looking through the wrong end of a telescope. Everything in front of me is shrinking as I move toward it and it is as though I am walking through a thick web of cotton. This has to be a dream, I think. This is not something that's supposed to be happening to me.

Then, in my periphery—and as I make my way to the bench to sit down next to this man who has beckoned me to him—I see what appears to be someone lying on one of the other metal benches in the cell. The thin blanket that covers him is moving. His pale arm dangles off the bench and his scabrous hand lightly brushes the concrete floor. Then I see the blanket move again as the man sits himself up and it falls into his lap, pooling around him as he blinks his eyes against the light.

And I know right away who he is.

He is skinnier now than I remember him, his eyes sunken into his pale face, deep circles like bruises underneath them and puffy bags of flesh that make it look as though he hadn't slept in months. His once-dark beard is streaked with gray now and is stragglier than it used to be, much longer too. It grows down almost to the middle of his sunken-in chest.

His clothes look like so many filthy rags dangling from his body and his hair is patchy in places where once it had been thick and wavy. But it is still him.

It is Father.

I stop right there in the middle of the cell. Everyone is watching me, waiting for me to do something, it seems.

Then the man beckoning me with his painted nails and his pouty lips, his tongue piercing, and his sickening voice, his smile once again fading as he too looks over at the figure who has by now started to rise from the heap of blankets and to stand up from the bench.

"Leave him alone," Father says.

"Fuck you, old man."

Father moves toward him. And as skinny as he has gotten, even with the dirty rags that serve as his clothes and that are draped over his gaunt frame like moss on a tree branch, his figure is still somehow imposing in here. The fluorescent light casts his shadow across the cement floor, which covers my own entirely now, enveloping it as though it is swallowing me whole.

"I don't think so," Father says. His voice sounds gravelly but still

strong, as it had when he preached to us from his dais at the front of
Light of His Way all those years ago.

He moves slightly. I can tell he's drunk, or hung over, his knees
wobbling and his arms outstretched for balance, but then—and as
though someone has flicked a switch inside of him—Father stands
straight and steady.

Then he walks between where I am standing and where the man
with the nail polish is starting to get up from his bench. Father stops
between us, a certain energy seeming to flow through him now,
straightening out his limbs, the arch of his back. It is as if a great
surge of electricity is flowing through his body.

Father gets close to this man and puts his face right next to his.
Looks him in the eyes. Seems to look through them. And I can
remember that look from when I was a kid and living with him on
the Acre, how it had the power to wilt someone down to nothing.

Then I see him reach into his jacket and pull out a knife from a
hidden slit in the side, just near his ribcage. He's standing so close to
this other man that I don't know if anyone else sees it. But I can. And
I swear it looks like the same knife he had used at the hamburger
place to cut that man's throat that time—the same knife I had won
at the fair, the one my dad used to slash Mr. Tally's tires. All these
pieces of my life are starting to swirl into place, like the planchette on
a Ouija board moving to spell out an important message that I can't
understand.

I think about what Father told us in church about that kid Billy
Milgrew. The boy he killed in juvenile detention hall. And I wonder if
he is he going to kill this person here too. I remember he had only cut
that man at the hamburger place, how he and his buddies scattered
off into the woods and Paul had come back with us to the Acre, only
to disappear himself that same day, never to be seen again.

None of this is making any sense, no matter how much I want it
to. And I still can't understand how Father got that knife in here in
the first place—past all the guards and the metal detectors. Maybe
they didn't search drunks like him that carefully. Just threw them in a
cell until they sobered up.

It doesn't matter anyway, because now the man who has been

trying to lure me over to him seems to shrink before Father and that knife, which is jabbed slightly into his side—not enough to even break through his sweater, but poking him nonetheless. He just pulls away from it, sits back down. Tries to laugh it off. "Fuck both y'all motherfuckers," he says.

Father turns toward me then. His blue eyes—despite being sunken into his now-gaunt face, resting above two bruise-colored crescents from too much cheap whiskey or not enough sleep or a combination of the two—lock with mine. I can see him sliding the knife back into the slit in the inside of his jacket.

I want to sit down, but there is still nowhere to sit. And suddenly everything in the jail cell seems to just fall away. The men standing at the front with their arms dangling out of the bars, ropes of cigarette smoke leaking into the corridor like tendrils of hair underwater. The TV, the crackling late-night talk show. The guards. Everything. It all just goes away.

Except for Father.

"Are you all right?" he says.

I can't make myself say anything, so I just nod my head yes.

"Good," he says. "Don't let people like him take advantage of you. This place is full of them, but men like him are ultimately weak. Powerless."

He speaks of that man as though he no longer even exists, as though he weren't just sitting down right behind him, could run a shank through his back if he wanted to.

Father keeps his eyes locked onto mine, and whether he recognizes me or not, I still can't tell. I just stand there. Frozen.

Then a loud buzzer sounds overhead and the cell door slides open on its heavy tracks.

"Woodbine," comes a voice from just outside the door. It's the guard who put me in here earlier.

"Time to make your phone call," he says.

I look over at Father one more time—in part to be sure that I had really seen him—but just that fast he has already started to slouch back toward his mound of blankets on the metal bench. His long greasy hair is hanging over his face so that I can no longer see his eyes, and all the energy that just seconds ago was coursing through him has dissipated. As quickly as a light whose wiring has been clipped.

I turn back to the front of the jail cell and start to make my way to where the guard is holding open the barred door for me. Waiting. Then I look one more time to where Father has gone back to his bench. He has already covered himself and I can see only that mound of blankets again, slowly rising up and down with his breathing.

Then the guard steps aside and nudges me through the opening and out into the corridor, closes the cell door and turns the large metal key to lock it back. He slowly clips the key to a ring on his belt, sighing with the effort. It's been a long night.

ACKNOWLEDGMENTS

The author wishes to express his sincere gratitude to J. Bruce Fuller, Diane Payne, Dixon Hearne, and the folks at the Sewanee Writers' Conference for reading early drafts and offering advice. He would also like to thank the editorial team at *The Peauxdunque Review*, Tad Bartlett, Emily Choate, Larry Wormington, and Maurice Carlos Ruffin, for publishing an early excerpt of the novel. Last, a degree of thanks is owed to the Southeastern Louisiana University Department of English for their support and camaraderie.